DIM THUNDER

Also by William Campbell Gault

ROUGH ROAD TO GLORY

BRUCE BENEDICT, HALFBACK

SPEEDWAY CHALLENGE

MR. QUARTERBACK

GALLANT COLT

MR. FULLBACK

THUNDER ROAD

E·P·DUTTON&CO.INC
EST. 1852
OVER 100 YEARS OF CREATIVE PUBLISHING

THUNDER

WILLIAM CAMPBELL GAULT

Illustrated by Edwin A. Butterfield, Jr.

E. P. DUTTON & CO., INC.

NEW YORK, 1958

For LEE SHIRVANIAN

ONE

It was quite a year. Some of the things I remember because they were close to me and important to me. I was young, that year, and some things that were important to me then don't seem quite so important now. But the things and the people that were close will be close to me forever. Like Chip.

Big things happened that year. Mark Twain died, just the man, not the legend nor the magic he left in print. Johnson whipped Jeffries, and the Los Angeles *Times* was wrecked in an explosion. On Sagamore Hill, Teddy Roosevelt, the great Colonel, sulked, because the man who had succeeded him in the White House, the man *he* had elected with his own deft efforts, was failing in his job.

At least, Teddy thought so. And Taft, the man in the White House, that pleasant, ponderous, unhappy man, must have agreed. It was a time of politics, as always, and a time of change. It was politics, now that I think of it, that started Chip and me on the road. I mean, politics was the straw. I guess there wasn't *anything* that would have prevented that. It was sort of our destiny, I suppose.

Yes, it was a time of change. There were almost a

half million cars on the road, but the horse was still mighty well respected. Glenn Curtiss flew from Albany to New York in the fragile, unpredictable thing called the airplane, winning for his feat ten thousand dollars.

And Mary Baker Eddy died, and Amundsen reached the South Pole. Booth Tarkington was well thought of, and he still looks all right to me, though there are some. . . . Well, that's another story.

This story is mostly about Chip and me. Or maybe, it's mostly about Chip. And it's about cars, which we both loved.

They said Chip was wild and a dreamer, and he was. They said he had too much imagination and not the proper respect for tradition, and that's true—if you think a person can have too much imagination, and respect for tradition is proper.

This man Taylor—Frederick Winslow Taylor—was causing quite a storm along the tradition trail with his theories of "scientific management." A few years later, Henry Ford was going to startle some of the die-hards with a flat five dollars a day, minimum. So it might be better to judge Chip from *now*, not *then*.

This much I know. He was a good friend, he had courage, he had the dream. He wasn't too big, but he had energy, fire, and daring. He lived with trouble, often, but it never rode him. He was one of the finest drivers I have ever seen, and I've seen them all, through the years.

He was a thin and wiry lad, with an engaging grin and stiff, coal-black hair, and he lived in the biggest house in town. His dad was a lawyer, and a good one. His dad was a "stand-patter" Republican and a firm one. He naturally expected Chip would share both the profession and the viewpoint, at the proper time.

His dad also had a Pierce Arrow, and that Chip was willing to share. They don't make them, any more, but when they did, they knew only one way, the best way, and it's a shame they had to die.

I didn't live in a big house, nor in town. I lived on the edge of town, in a little house, and I had a bicycle shop in front of the house. I did some auto-repairing, on the side, and made enough to support Mom and me. There were just the two of us.

It was a good dirt road in front, and some of the blades of the day seemed to think it was a speedway. That's where they tried out their Reos and their Nationals, their Hupmobiles and their Marmons. Mom didn't like it. Mom said that was all right on a track, or a supervised road race, and a thrilling sight it was under those circumstances. But it wasn't right on a public road, and particularly where there were so many spirited horses. The lovers of that animal used the road, too, for their faster steeds.

I agreed with Mom. I usually did.

It was a spring day, I remember, when I first saw the Pierce coming along the road. The young fellow behind the wheel was leaning out over the door, listening to the motor, and looking displeased. I think of him now as young, but he was my own age. I'd been on my own for three years, and he was still in school, and looked it.

He saw my sign, and stopped the car, but left the motor running. "Listen," he said.

We both listened.

Chug, chug, chug, the motor said, in its steady way, in its lordly way, *chug, chug, chug.*

"Sounds all right to me," I said.

He frowned, and his dark blue eyes were thoughtful. "Well, maybe—wait—" and he climbed in behind the wheel.

He accelerated the motor, and the chug quickened, still steady, still smooth. But there'd been just a fraction of hesitation.

"Timing?" I asked.

He shook his head. He took his gauntlets off, and came down to lift the hood.

"I think it's the carburetor," he said. "They should put the carburetor *above* the motor, so the gas falls, instead of being sucked up."

I didn't think of what he said, at the time. But thinking of it now, he meant a down-draft carbu-

14

retor, and that's what they did do—twenty years later, or so.

"Maybe she's starving out," I said. "How is she at high speed?"

"She's kind of rough, at sixty," he said.

I stared at him. "Sixty—?" It didn't mean much, even two or three years later, but at the time . . . "Sixty—?" I repeated.

He smiled that cocky smile of his. "C'mon over to the fair grounds. I'll show you."

"I believe you," I said. "Well, let's take the carburetor off, and see. Maybe it's dirty, or maybe bigger jets—"

We worked together, taking off the carburetor. He was a good man to work with. We took it into the shop and that's where the friendship began. He wanted to get a car of his own, I learned, a car he could strip down and step up—for racing.

I told him I'd had those dreams myself.

"Hey," he said, "maybe, if we worked together—" He grinned. "My name is Adams, Tom Adams, but everybody calls me Chip. What's your name?"

"Elmer," I told him sadly, "and everybody calls me that, too."

He laughed, and said, "What kind of car were you thinking of buying?"

"There's a Marmon," I told him, "a fellow up the road smashed up in an accident. Body's kind of shot, but the frame's true, and the motor wasn't hurt a bit. I was thinking, if I geared it up, and took off the fenders—"

His eyes were beginning to shine. "Could we—could you undersling it, you think?"

"Maybe. I—well, I couldn't buy it, right now. Things are kind of tight, right now."

He nodded. "And I wouldn't want to use Dad's money for mine. Dad isn't so—keen on this automobile bug of mine." He shook his head. "He's got me going to law school."

"I've heard of your father," I said. "I guess he did all right with his law."

"Sure, but it's not for me." He seemed to shake himself. "Let's see if we can't ream that jet out with something."

When we put the carburetor back on the Pierce, it seemed like the hesitation was gone, like the deep-throated rumble was almost instantaneous with the opening throttle.

He was putting his goggles back on, and his duster. "I'll try her out. Want to go along?"

I wanted to. But I had to watch the shop, I told him.

"I'll tell you what," he said. "I'll try her out, and then I'll come back and watch the shop while you try her out. Okay—Elm?"

"Okay," I agreed quickly, and wondered why nobody had thought of that fine nickname until now.

I watched him drive off. I watched him until the Pierce was just a cloud of dust on the sunny road. I turned, then, to see Mom watching from the front porch.

"Fix him up, Elmer?" she called.

"Think so, Mom. That's Judge Adams' boy." He wasn't a judge, but he was the kind everyone would call "judge."

"Mighty big car for a slim young man," Mom commented, and went back into the house. I guess Mom measured all the young men by me, and I was two inches over six feet.

When Chip brought the car back, he was grinning. "It's like a dream," he said. "You're a fine mechanic."

I took it out, and it was like a dream. No fluid drive, you understand, or floating power. Not much by today's standards, not even a starter—they were just coming out. But a Pierce, and a part of that day's magic.

The sun was warm, and the road wound between the flanking trees. I'd never driven a car as fine as this before; I think it must have been right then I decided cars were my life.

It isn't all of it clear, now. Some things are dim,

some are vivid. But I remember that ride, and coming back to the shop. I remember talking to Chip. He didn't seem in any hurry to leave.

He told me they were laying a permanent surface on the big track at Indianapolis, and that a five hundred mile race was being planned for next year. We talked about Joe Dawson and Barney Oldfield, about Ray Harroun and Ralph DePalma. Somehow, the talk came back to the Marmon up the road, and somehow it developed that when the time came, we'd buy it together, and race it, together.

Mom was making doughnuts, and she brought some down to the shop, about the middle of the afternoon. She brought a pitcher of milk, too, and some glasses.

We ate all the doughnuts, and talked some more. About the new self-starters that were coming out, and what a change that would make. The horse, we decided, was doomed—especially for racing. Who'd want to watch a race as slow as that, in the future?

Then Mom came to call me for supper, and Chip left. I can still see the Pierce going slowly down the road to town. I can still hear him singing, "Yip-I-Addy-I-Ay."

Summer came on. Teddy came back from Europe, and retreated into the quiet of his early private life. Taft was helpless against the battles of the Insurgents and the Stand-patters, but the Colonel issued no statement in support of either side, nor any criticism of Taft.

The same can't be said for Chip's dad. He had, since the instigation of the new amendment to the Constitution, taken an unreasonable dislike to Taft.

This amendment was the proposed income tax, and to Judge Adams it meant a persecution of the moneyed classes. The Republican party, the Judge stated for the local press, was in danger of a permanent and disastrous split. And all because of men like Dolliver and La Follette, Norris and Beveridge. If Aldrich and Cannon couldn't handle these men in their respective houses, it was time Teddy came back into public life.

It was one of the Colonel's virtues, I recall, that he could appeal to all men, in all classes, without a loss of personal integrity.

Politics didn't mean much to Chip and me, only so far as it affected his dad's disposition, which, as the summer wore on, grew progressively worse.

In July, Chip took a job with the bicycle factory at the edge of town. He told me about it right away.

I said, "Your dad isn't going to like that."

"I haven't told him, yet," he said. "Elm—do you think I'm being—I mean, do you think it's wrong to disobey, if you feel sure inside of you—" He broke off. "Oh, you know what I mean."

"You mean," I asked him, "that you and your dad aren't getting along?"

"That's right. When Mother was alive, she kept peace, but it's different, now. We seem to be—on edge all the time. I told him yesterday I wasn't going back to law school this fall."

"Why not?"

He stared at me. "You know why. Motors, automobiles—that's my life. I'd never make a good lawyer. I haven't the patience, or the dignity—or the sense. I want to be an engineer, Elm."

I shook my head. "I don't know what to tell you, Chip. I was always taught not to disobey. I never wanted to, since I was knee-high to a grasshopper."

"But your mom's different," he protested. "She lets you do about anything you want to do."

"Well," I compromised, "you're earning your keep, now. Maybe your dad won't be so strict with you."

It was late in that same month, that Judge Adams came out to the shop. I thought it was Chip, at first, though he hadn't been using the car on his recent trips out. When I saw the broad, stern face of Judge Adams, though, I knew he wasn't dropping in to pass the time of day.

He stood in the doorway of the shop and asked if I was Elmer Ryan.

I said I was.

"Is your mother home?"

"Yes, sir," I said. "She's up at the house. Matter of fact, sir, she's sitting on the porch, there, right now."

"Thank you," he said gravely. "My business is with her, but I don't mind telling you, young man, that it's about you, and the influence you've had on my son."

I said nothing. I gulped. I felt like a big, dumb lout.

He looked around the shop, before speaking again. "I am sure this trade suits you admirably, Mr. Ryan, and honest work is nothing to be ashamed of. However, I hadn't planned it as a trade for my son. Do you understand that?"

"I do, sir," I said, "and I hadn't planned it as a trade for your son, either. I think he's old enough to make his own decisions, just like I am."

He colored a little and seemed to stiffen. "I'll discuss *that* with your mother, young man," he said.

"Yes, sir," I said, and went back to the bike I was working on.

But as soon as he'd left, and started for the porch, I went around to the back part of the shop, where I could watch them.

Mom was reading a magazine, and drinking lemonade. I saw the Judge go up on the porch and take off his cap. I saw him sit down in the rocker, across from Mom's.

But I couldn't hear a word they said.

A little later, the Judge came down the steps again. He looked furious. Mom was standing on the porch, and she didn't look in the best of humor, either.

I heard the Pierce start with a bang, and then roar off. I went up to the porch where Mom still stood, glaring down the road where the Pierce threw dust into the afternoon sunlight.

She finally saw me standing there. "He's a stubborn man," she said.

"He wants Chip to be a lawyer, Mom," I explained. "Chip's his only child, and the Judge is disappointed in him."

"A boy," Mom said firmly, "will be what God and the boy's own nature determine he will be. And a man as learned as Judge Adams should certainly know that."

Then she went back to the rocker, and I went back to the shop.

Chip came out before supper, on his bike. He seemed embarrassed. He wanted to know what his dad had said to Mom.

I told him I didn't know, exactly. I told him what his dad had said to me.

He said, "I'm leaving home, Elm. I'm going to get a room, somewhere near the plant, and make my own way."

I didn't feel qualified to offer any advice on that. I said, "Why don't you talk it over with Mom? She'll tell you what to do."

"All right," he said. "All right." He seemed relieved that the decision wouldn't be completely his.

He didn't come back to the shop. When I went up to the house for supper, he was with Mom in the kitchen. He was sitting there on a chair near the window, looking thoughtful.

Mom said, "Chip's decided to stay with us, Elmer." She brushed at one eye with the back of her hand. "Nothing's decided *for sure,* but we think it will be best that way, for a while."

It was a terrible meal. All of us looked down at our plates and didn't say a word. I wondered what Judge Adams would do when he found out Chip wasn't going to live at home. If I had only one son, I know what I'd do. But I wasn't Judge Adams, and could never be.

Chip didn't even go back to get his clothes. They weren't his, he said. From now on, nothing would be his he didn't earn. He looked terribly grim when he said that, and not at all young, any more.

Mom fixed a lunch for him to carry, next morning, and stood on the porch and watched him go off to work on his bike. When she came into the house, she looked like she was going to cry.

"That poor, brave boy," she said.

"He's only doing what I've been doing for three years," I pointed out, "working for a living."

"It's not the same, Elmer Ryan," she said stoutly. "He's so—so little."

He was five feet, eight inches, strong as a mule, intelligent, and handy with his hands. But he would always bring out that protective instinct in women. Maybe it was that stiff, unruly hair, or the brilliant blue eyes. Maybe it was because he always seemed to be fighting something that looked too big for him.

I said, "Well, the Judge will be out here today, and things will pop."

"I've nothing to say to Judge Adams," Mom said.

And Judge Adams, it appeared, had nothing to say to us.

It was a bad time. There wasn't anything I could get Chip interested in. He worked ten hours a day, six days a week, and he was usually too tired, at night, to be much company. Mom was unhappy about the whole situation, though she tried to forget it by thinking of how unfair the Judge had been.

Then, one night, I said, "You got any money, Chip?"

"A little," he answered. "Do you need it, Elm?"

"I was thinking about that Marmon," I said. "It's

still there, and it ought to be pretty reasonable, **by** now."

The blue eyes brightened, I thought. And his voice had some life in it. "Say—you think— Look, we could work on it, nights, and—"

"That's what I was thinking," I agreed. "Give us something to do."

He was looking at the floor. "I haven't much money, though. On twelve a week, it's hard to save much. And I had clothes to buy."

"I'll go and dicker with him, tomorrow," I said. "If it's cheap enough, I'll buy it."

He nodded quickly, and his eyes were as brilliant as ever. "I hear they're going to have an automobile race at the fair this year. Elm, we could get it ready by then."

"We'll see," I said. "We can try."

When I went to bed that night, I could hear him, through the thin wall that separated our rooms. He was humming *Waltz Me Around Again, Willie.*

Old New Anderson, who owned the Marmon, was known throughout the county as the shrewdest horse trader and handiest farmer of his day. Getting anything from him, and getting it cheaply, was something only a foolhardy and determined youth would attempt. Well, I was determined enough, I can't say about the other.

He was out in the stable, repairing some harness

25

when I wheeled my bicycle into his yard, the next morning.

He was a thin, lanky man with a perpetually unhappy face, and suspicion in his small, dark eyes. "I reckon you came to see about the automobile," he said, as an opening gambit.

I admitted it. "I figured it was about time you had it fixed."

I thought he looked faintly disappointed.

"Fixed?" he said doubtfully. "You aiming to make a few dollars, fixing it up, young man?"

"No harm in trying," I said innocently. "I'm trying to build up the automobile end of my business. You see, Mr. Anderson, the longer that car sits out in the weather like that, the more it will rust. Well, that might not hurt the outside, so much. But if it rusts inside the motor, in the cylinders, and weakens them, why, it'd be nothing but junk, and—"

"Whoa," he said suddenly. "Take it easy, there, boy. I see what you're trying to do. You're trying to run that car down, so you can buy it cheap."

I stared at him. "Buy it—? With what, Mr. Anderson? I haven't the kind of money that car is worth. That's a Marmon, sir, and way out of my class."

He couldn't figure that one out. He looked mighty puzzled, for a few moments.

I went on. "Why, a few hundred dollars will fix that car up, I'd bet, almost as good as new."

"Would it, now? And then what would I have?"

"You'd have a car anybody would want to buy," I said. "Of course, I'll be honest with you, sir, you could probably sell it, right now, the way it is. But you wouldn't get its proper value."

He was chewing his lower lip, and studying me. Finally, he said, "I suppose you could run it down to your shop and take it apart. You could tell better, maybe, after that, how much it would cost to get it ready to sell, eh?"

"I'd be glad to give you a free estimate," I said solemnly. "If we pushed it out to the road, I could almost coast it all the way to the shop."

"Coast—?" he said. "There's nothing wrong with it, but the body. Crank 'er up, and run 'er down, lad."

I shook my head gravely. "I'm afraid to."

The dark eyes were hard with suspicion. "Afraid to? What are you trying to tell me?"

"If those cylinder walls are weak, if they've been rusted through—" I shook my head.

"Well," he said irritably, "and what if they are?"

"She'll explode," I said, and met his gaze squarely.

His head jerked back, and he stared at me. "Explode—? Are you serious, boy?"

I nodded. "I am, Mr. Anderson. I've seen it happen. It's—" Again, I shook my head.

His eyes left my face and wandered around the stable, to the various stalls, and the animals there. I could almost see the gears and wheels revolving in his brain. Horses, he must be thinking, don't *explode*. Horses don't rust, or have flat tires. A man can sell a horse, at a reasonable profit, if he has the knack.

Horses, Ned Anderson could understand. Horses and men. But these confounded automobiles, ... I saw the craftiness coming to his face.

"Of course," he said, "we don't know, do we, whether or not it's rusted inside?"

"We don't," I admitted.

"Once you get it down to that shop of yours, and get it apart, you'll know, won't you?"

I nodded.

"And if it's true, if it's rusted—?"

"You can always sell it for the scrap value. Lot of iron there."

"Of course." I thought he winced a little, but he was smiling his tight smile when he continued. "You a gambler, boy?"

"No, sir."

"Nonsense," he said irritably, "everything's a gamble. Why, in your business, that's what you're doing, gambling on the future."

"Well," I admitted, "I suppose I'm a gambler, in that way."

The smile came back. "Of course. And you kind of like that car, don't you? Admit it, now."

I nodded sadly. "But I'm a poor man, Mr. Anderson. And Mom would never let me keep the car. She'd make me sell it."

"But at a profit, eh? I'll bet you're handy with a wrench, young man. I'll bet you could make that car as good as new."

I said nothing.

He coughed. "So we don't know it's rusted. And you *are* a gambler. So, what's it worth to you, right now, before we push it out onto the road?"

I scratched my head, and appeared to be figuring. I knew that he had got it in a trade involving some horses, and I knew he wouldn't risk really valuable horses in a trade for anything as financially unstable as an automobile. But I couldn't arrive at a figure, without knowing what was in his mind, first.

I said, finally, "I just can't figure it, Mr. Anderson."

He was chewing his lip again. He didn't want to name any figure, either, I knew. Then he said cautiously, "Would three hundred dollars be a reasonable figure, just as she stands?"

I said, "It's worth that, I'm sure, if the cylinder walls aren't rusted too badly, but for resale, if Mom makes me sell it—"

He said nothing, waiting.

Finally, I said, "How would this be? I'll give you a hundred and fifty. If Mom makes me sell it, and it *can be sold*, I'll give you half the profit on that, minus what money and time I'd have to put into it, of course."

He thought about that for what seemed to be a long time. Then he looked around again at his horses, those creatures he could understand. "All right, it's a deal, like that." We shook hands.

He did better than push me out to the road. He hitched up a team, and towed me all the way to the shop. I got the money from Mom, and paid him.

He counted it all carefully, and said, "We won't need any written agreement about that reselling business, young man. I know your reputation." He looked around at my tools, at my tire repairing outfit, at my stock of fan belts and oil and grease. The smile that came to his thin face was almost fatherly. "Young fellow," he said kindly enough, "I wish you a lot of success. But I can't help but feel you're in a troublesome business."

I agreed that might be. I said, "But I never was much of a hand with horses, Mr. Anderson. I'll just have to make out the best I can."

He left, and I heard the clop of his horses' hoofs getting dimmer and dimmer, while I stood there, glowing. I had a *Marmon*. *We* had a Marmon, Chip and I . . . .

It was a runabout, and sporty. It had a four-and-a-half-inch bore and a five-inch stroke, a six-cylinder job. It was a duplicate of the Marmon motor Ray Harroun had in his car, 447.1 cubic inches of piston displacement. Ray drove his to victory in the first 500 at Indianapolis that next year at an average speed of 74.59 miles an hour. For five hundred miles, that's moving.

I must have just looked at it, for five minutes. Then I went to work, pulling off the head.

When Chip came home, I was still working on it. He didn't say much when he saw it, but he seemed to be a new man, after that. We worked on it together until late that night. We pulled the motor out, and took the fenders off.

Around midnight, we stopped. I blew out two of the shop's three lanterns. The other hung directly over the car, on a nail, and Chip seemed loath to put it out. He was staring at the car.

I came over to stand next to him. Finally, he said, "I never asked you how much, Elm."

"I stole it," I said, "and I'm ashamed of myself, a little. A hundred and fifty dollars. And from a horse trader."

"You stole it," he agreed. "Golly—I'm happy—almost."

He turned down the wick on the last lamp, and blew it out. In the dark, he said, "Elm, I'm sure glad I met you. A Marmon, gosh."

We were quiet, walking to the house, so as not to disturb Mom.

TWO

It was a hot and humid summer. We didn't mind, though. Chip would come home late from the bicycle factory, thin and pale, but his eyes were alive, and his mind full of ideas about dressing up the car. Oh, we worked, and planned and dreamed . . . .

Judge Adams was getting a lot of publicity. The Judge, at his own expense and without the sanction of the local committee, was waging a one-man crusade to save the Republican party. He was indignant at Teddy's continued silence, and his allegiance was shifting to Taft. Taft, to the Judge, represented the party and the Judge was a party man. It was the Insurgents who drew his wrath, not the Democrats.

The Judge's crusade must have been a topic of conversation in every house in the county. Every house but ours. Chip never mentioned him, and until Chip did, Mom and I wouldn't.

By early fall, the Marmon was ready.

But there would be no race at the fairgrounds. The fair had always been the mecca of the harness racers, and it was the harness racers who objected to giving up the track to the automobiles. Not only would it take away one of their limited racing days,

35

but they feared the effects of those spinning wheels on the track's surface.

The fair board met, to consider all the factors. They could get an A.A.A. sanction if they ran the auto race, and a Triple-A sanction would attract the best in the game. But the benefits of that were not enough to outweigh the almost guaranteed attendance power of the pacers and trotters. There would be no race at the fairgrounds.

But there would be an automobile race. As an added attraction for the crowd that would be in town that week, there would be a road race. And the road would be the one which ran past our house. The race would start about four hundred yards from our house and would circle back on a side road to the starting point.

The night we learned this, we finished our work on the car. Chip said, "If we get up early tomorrow, the road will be clear. Say, around four o'clock?"

It was our first trip, and Chip drove. We made one trip, loafing, and then Chip said, "You take it, for the next one."

I shook my head. "I like the way you handle her."

We didn't loaf on the second trip. That Marmon was a road-hugging, spirited sweetheart, and Chip let her talk. She talked very well. He came into the last curve, broadsiding, and I should have been scared, but I wasn't. Because the Marmon and Chip were a combination, and I knew it, that first day. I would be the man with the wrench.

When we chugged into the yard again, I told him this.

"Oh, no," Chip said. "This is fifty-fifty. You've got as much right to drive as I have. More, in fact. I'm not going to take *that* away from you, Elm."

"You're not taking a thing away from me," I said. "Later, maybe, after I've had more experience, I'll change off with you. But we've only got a week. I can't learn what you know, not in a week."

We tried it out a few more mornings on the same road. The second morning, we got some competition. It was a National, a racing job, and it pulled up even with us, as we slued out of the first curve.

Chip fed the Marmon all she'd take.

That National was roaring like a demon, and its big wooden-spoked wheels were throwing a whirlwind of dust and pebbles as it dug for traction.

This man was no local sport with a homemade speed wagon. He was one of the giants, I felt sure, here for the road race.

Chip didn't give an inch. That Marmon's thunder was a match for the National's and Chip's courage and confidence would waver before no man's prestige.

We roared down that country road, pacing it out. Chip was smiling, his eyes narrowed beneath his goggles, squinting into the early morning sun. I felt just a bit uneasy, for the first time.

Hub and hub down that narrow road, only inches from the ditch, shaking the morning with our thunder, covering the fields with dust. And the National didn't gain an inch.

Ahead, another curve loomed closer, a curve to the left.

We were in the right-hand lane. We would have to drop behind for the turn for the National had the inside track. And nobody would dare take an unbanked curve to the left, not from the right-hand lane, not under competition.

The Marmon didn't cut down.

I looked over at Chip, and the smile was still there. I gripped the side of my seat, and watched the National.

It was still logging; it was still keeping abreast.

The barn that flanked the oncoming curve grew bigger and bigger as we bore down on it. I thought we gained a little on the National, but I couldn't be sure. I didn't want to take my eyes from the road ahead, not at the moment.

The barn was clear, now, every detail of it. Chip found another r.p.m. somewhere in that big, straining motor, and the Marmon began to edge faintly to the right, covering the few inches of clearance we still had on that side.

Then that thundering sweetheart seemed to leap, as Chip swung the wheel sharply to the left.

I tensed, waiting. Waiting for a screeching tire to burst, waiting for the smash that would mean we had slammed into the National. The tires held, as we broadsided out of the turn.

And the National, I was surprised to discover, trailed us. We had adequate clearance. It trailed us all the way, from there on, pressing us, edging up, but trailing, all the way.

When we pulled into the yard, some minutes later, it still trailed us. And as Chip snapped off the ignition, the chug of the National died, too.

The man sitting behind the wheel had his goggles up as we climbed from the Marmon. He was grinning.

"Nice work, boy," he said.

Chip gulped, and looked at me. But I was looking at the man in the National. It was Howard Wilcox. It was one of the giants, all right.

Chip said, "Gosh, Mr. Wilcox, if I'd known it was you—"

"I wish you had," he said, "if you feel that way about me. I'd have saved some gray hair." He climbed from the car. "That's a Marmon Wasp, isn't it?"

Chip nodded. "And I'm Chip Adams. This is Elmer Ryan, Mr. Wilcox."

39

He shook hands with both of us. He told us our motor was a replica of Ray Harroun's, which we knew. He told us Ray had an innovation on his Marmon, a rear view mirror. It was one of those simple ideas, but nobody had ever thought of it before.

Joe Dawson, he told us, was driving a Marmon too, that year, but a four-cylinder job. Joe would be here for the race, as would Ralph DePalma.

"DePalma—?" Chip said, and looked at me. "We'll be in fast company, Elm."

Wilcox put a friendly hand on Chip's shoulder. "Treat 'em like you treated me, boy, and you won't need to worry. You've done a lot of racing, I can tell that."

Before Chip could answer, Mom called from the porch, "Are you boys going to gab all morning? Because, if you are, I can throw away these hot cakes."

"You got enough for three of us, Mom?" I asked.

"I've enough for Coxey's Army," Mom said. "Will you hurry? They're no good unless they're hot, you know."

When we introduced Howard Wilcox to Mom, even she was impressed. He was one of the great road racers of his day, perhaps the greatest.

But he ate just as many of Mom's pancakes as an ordinary human being. He told us how he'd broken in, as a mechanic, only the year before. But being a mechanic wasn't enough, even a riding mechanic.

He was sorry to hear, he said, that the fairground authorities hadn't permitted the use of the track. Mom agreed with him on that. "A man," she affirmed, "has a right to risk his neck, if that's his choice. But too many spectators are getting hurt in these road races. The track's the place for racing cars."

"That Indianapolis will be the place," Wilcox said. "You watch me win that one, next year."

It so happened he didn't win it. Not until 1919, though he was in there, giving them trouble every year.

Chip went to work, and Wilcox back to town, and I went down to the shop. I wasn't down there for more than an hour, when Mom came down.

"Elmer," she said, "I'm worried."

"About the race, Mom?"

"Only partly. I've been thinking about Chip and the Judge. I've been thinking, with things the way they are, Chip is my responsibility."

"He isn't, though. He's just living with us, and paying board, Mom."

She was quiet. She was looking out at the Marmon in the yard. Finally, she said, "You boys love that contraption out there, don't you? It's your whole life."

"It's pretty important to us, all right."

She sighed. "Then I won't make the mistake of fighting it." I could see her eyes were wet. "I won't let it come between me—and my boys."

I took her in my arms. She was sniffling, a little, and that's not like Mom. "It's a heck of a looking thing, Mom," I said, "but I guess it represents progress. Nobody ever got anywhere fighting progress."

"I suppose not," she said, and wiped her eyes with her apron. "But you be careful, Elmer Ryan. You be as careful as anyone can be in that thing."

"Sure," I promised. "Of course." And I wondered just how careful a man could be in one of those things—and still win a race.

When I went up to the house for lunch, Mom seemed normal. At any rate she was humming as she worked at the stove. She told me she'd seen some men driving stakes into the field near the curve, up the road.

"They'll probably stake out all the curves," I guessed, "and keep the crowds behind them. That's where spectators can get hurt."

Mom looked at me. She was thinking, probably, that that's where the drivers get hurt, too, and the riding mechanics. But she didn't say a word. She'd said what she had to say, this morning, and she wasn't one to belabor a point. A very unusual woman, Mom.

Chip was sure full of ambition when he came

home from work, that night. And full of ideas. He wanted to cut down the head on the Marmon, increase the compression and add another gas tank. He wanted to gear it still higher.

We didn't have time, and I told him so. The race was only four days off. We couldn't take a chance on anything now; we wouldn't be able to fully test anything new, in that time.

"But look at the field," he protested, "Dawson and DePalma and Howard Wilcox."

"All here but Barney Oldfield," I admitted. Barney was still more interested in motorcycles, that year.

"And you think the Marmon's good enough for that gang?" Chip asked me.

"I think it is."

He was still looking at me, a question in his eyes.

"And I think you are, too," I said. "You're not scared, Chip?"

"A little," he admitted. "Aren't you?"

I nodded.

"We've got our nerve," he said, "running a hundred and fifty dollar gas-buggy against that field."

"We've got our nerve," I agreed, "and it's one thing we don't want to lose."

We still made the early morning runs, but not at any record speeds. We just breezed, feeling the curves, noting the narrow spots, planning our strategy. Behind the wheel Chip seemed content enough, but the inactivity of our nights made him restless as a dog with fleas.

The day before the race, he asked, "How would you like to go to a party tonight?"

"What kind of party?"

"A dance—at Hunter's." He was grinning.

"You know I don't dance," I said. "And the Hunters are way out of my class, Chip."

"All right," he said. "We won't go, then."

"You can go," I protested. "It's *you* they asked. They're your friends, Chip."

"Forget it," he said. "If you don't like them—"

"All right," I said. "I'll go. And when your friends ask why I'm not dancing, you can tell them I'm just a hick, I never learned."

He nodded. "I'll tell them that." He grinned again. "Thanks, Elm. You'll see why I wanted to go when we get there."

The Hunters, he told me, were sending a man around to pick us up at eight o'clock.

How I hated to get ready the stiff collar, and the Sunday suit, and the scrubbing, scrubbing, scrubbing to get the grease out of the pores of my hands. Chip ignored my grumbling. He whistled while he was getting ready, as though he were having the time of his life.

44

We finished just as the Hunter's Stutz drove into the yard.

The Hunter home was a big, ornate, gabled mansion on the town's highest hill. It was one of the earliest homes in town to be converted completely to electricity, and every window seemed to be glaring with light as we drove up. My hopes for retiring to some dim corner and being lost during the party were shattered by this discovery. I could feel myself stiffen.

It wasn't a formal party, but it was a big one. I felt like the original country bumpkin in my Sunday suit, my five-year-old Sunday suit.

In the high reception hall, an angel waited, watching us approach. She was wearing a shimmering shade of blue, and she had a blue ribbon in her light hair. As Chip presented me, I learned that she was our hostess.

She was Elaine Hunter. This, I suspected, was why Chip wanted to come.

She said, "Chip's told me so much about you, Mr. Ryan, I feel like we're old friends. And we're going to be, aren't we?"

"I certainly hope so," I blurted. "I—" And then I realized I had nothing more to say. I could feel the color climb in my face.

She said, "As a matter of fact, I'd hoped that all

three of us could have a good talk, after the others have gone." Her voice grew more grave. "Dad particularly wants to see you, Chip."

I thought Chip stiffened. But all he said was, "I'll enjoy that, Elaine."

"I've saved the first dance for you, Chip," she said softly. "I've saved some others, too. I thought, perhaps—"

"I appreciate that," Chip said. "I haven't had much chance to see you lately, Elaine—"

I saw the way it was, then. I got the strangest feeling, a lonely, out-of-place feeling. I couldn't understand it.

I met some others, Chip's cousin, Harold Adams, a blond and quiet, polite young man. I had no reason to dislike him, but I did, the moment I met him. He was *too* polite and *too* quiet.

He said to Chip, "Your father asked me to have a talk with you, Chip, and I promised I would. Would tomorrow be all right?"

Chip answered, "Tomorrow night would." He smiled. "I'll be busy, most of the day."

Harold Adams frowned. "You're going to—race, tomorrow?"

Chip nodded.

His cousin was still frowning, and saying nothing.

"Tomorrow night all right?" Chip asked.

"I—suppose so. Yes, tomorrow night."

And as his cousin walked away, Chip said to me, "The fair-haired boy. *That's* what Dad wants me to be. *That's* Dad's idea of a model young man."

"I think he's nice," Elaine protested. "He's so polite, and gentlemanly. I've been—seeing quite a lot of him, Chip, since you, since—"

"I'm jealous," Chip said. He nudged me.

I met Jean Calvin, a tall, slender girl with dark hair and glowing, dark eyes. I liked her, on sight.

Elaine said, "Jean has saved the first dance for Mr. Ryan, at my request. Jean's my best friend."

Chip said, "Elm doesn't dance."

"In which case," Jean said, "we can talk. It's really too warm to dance, anyway." A tactful, comfortable girl, Jean Calvin.

So, while Elaine and Chip danced that first dance, while the orchestra played the *Blue Danube*, Jean Calvin and I sat on the immense, cool side porch, and talked.

I learned she was supporting the suffrage movement. She wanted to know if I'd seen Forbes-Robertson in *The Passing of the Third Floor Back*, if I'd read *The Rosary*, or seen Marie Dressler in *Tillie's Nightmare*.

And when I said a rather uncomfortable "No" to all of these, she asked, "Do you think a National is faster than a Stutz?"

I explained about that in some detail, and the first

dance was over before I was through. Her partner came to claim her for the second.

The evening passed easily enough, after that. I had a few more danceless dances with Jean before the party broke up. She told me she was coming out to sign up Mom; Mom was interested in the suffrage movement, but had never joined.

Then, after the guests had left, I sat in the huge, deserted ballroom with Elaine, while Chip was in her father's study.

She said, "Chip's breaking his father's heart with that racing business."

I couldn't think of anything to say to that.

She went on. "Harold tells me that it's the most dangerous sport in America, and leads to nothing. That's true, isn't it?"

"I don't know," I said. "It's a sort of testing ground for the automobile industry, I always thought. But Harold may be right."

She sighed. "I'm sure he's right. Harold's intelligent and he's—sensible."

Then Chip was coming along the ballroom floor, his gaze downward, his intent young face stormy. I knew the signs.

Elaine went to meet him. "You've decided, Chip," she said. "You're giving it up? You're not going to race tomorrow?"

He stopped, and looked at her for moments. "I'm going to race tomorrow."

She stood there quietly, the back of one hand to her mouth. She was trembling.

Chip said, "Elaine, please don't worry about me. I'm doing what I want to do. Everything's all right."

Her voice was little more than a whisper. "Good night, Chip. I won't say any more—" Then she was sobbing, and hurrying from the room.

The car was waiting for us out in front, and we rode home without any conversation at all. At the top of the stairs, he paused, and looked at me.

"Maybe I'm a fool," he said.

"I don't think so," I said, "but maybe we both are."

His grin was kind of weak.

I said, "That Elaine's a beautiful girl."

He nodded. "Well, good night, Elm. See you in the morning." Then he paused. "You know, I could ride alone, tomorrow. It's legal, either way."

"I want to be along," I said. "I wouldn't miss it."

He winked at me, and went down the hall to his room.

I had some trouble getting to sleep that night. I kept thinking about the field in tomorrow's race, and the way that road was graded. I kept remembering how it wasn't always possible to keep the crowd back where they belonged.

I thought of Elaine, and Jean Calvin. I hadn't known any girls of their class, before. But then, I hadn't known *many* girls of *any* class, before.

Mom didn't have much to say at breakfast, and neither did Chip. When he went out, to tinker with the car, Mom asked me, "What happened at the party last night?"

"I didn't dance, if that's what you mean," I answered.

"You know what I mean, Elmer," she said. "What happened to Chip?"

"His girl doesn't want him to race," I said.

"Girl—?" Mom said. "I didn't know he had one."

"Neither did I," I told her, "until last night." Then I changed the subject and told her about Jean Calvin.

"I'll be glad to have her visit us," Mom said. "She sounds like a sensible, modern girl."

I went out to help Chip tinker with the Marmon. Not that it needed it, not that it wasn't as ready as it would ever be, but it was something to occupy our minds.

The road had been busy most of the morning, with the crowds going to the fair. But it was being barricaded, now, and cleared of traffic. Already, some of the fans were hunting choice locations.

It wasn't a very long run, and for that reason, it

had been decided that a triple circuit of the entire route would make up the contest.

Right after lunch, Chip and I drove down to the starting line. There was another entry already there, a big four-cylinder Simplex. Ralph DePalma was behind the wheel.

Don't get the wrong idea about it being a four-cylinder job. No automobile motor in the world today, four, six, eight, twelve or sixteen cylinder, has as much displacement as that Simplex of Ralph DePalma's had. It had a total piston displacement of 597 cubic inches, a five and three-quarter inch bore and a five and three-quarter inch stroke, a so-called "square" motor. It was a lot of car, and one of the two best drivers in the world was behind the wheel.

Maybe Elaine had been right.

DePalma climbed from his juggernaut, as we rolled to a stop in the Marmon. "Howie told me about you boys," he greeted us. "My name's De-Palma."

As if we didn't know.

I suppose there should have been harps playing. I suppose there should have been some of that manna around, and ambrosia. Because we were in heaven, right then.

Chip snapped out of his slump, and those dark

51

blue eyes of his sparkled like diamonds. Joe Dawson, and his Marmon four, came along a little later, and Wilcox. There were others; I can't remember them all. Tommy Cavanaugh and Red Nelson. Bob Whitney. The smell of oil grew heavy on the hot air, and ahead, the road was lined with spectators, grouped at strategic spots, high spots.

The starter was Jeff Stuart. He lined us up two abreast, some hundreds of yards behind the starting post. It wasn't a "flying start," I suppose, but it was a "running start." It was Jeff's idea of the best way to get the monsters off.

All the motors were running now, chugging in that deep-throated rumble those big, wide-bore jobs all had. Dawson and DePalma and Wilcox, and the others. Among the others, in the third row, paired with Bob Whitney, sat yours truly and Chip Adams, apprentices in this dangerous and exciting trade.

Then the motor noise was growing, and the cars were moving forward, drumming toward the line, toward the flag in the hand of Jeff Stuart.

Directly ahead of us was Joe Dawson, Wilcox flanking him. In the spot of honor, in the first row, was Ralph DePalma, flanked by Red Nelson. Red was a heavy-footed giant who gave no quarter and expected none. Even DePalma would find Red no cinch. It was shaping up as a race to remember.

The flag flashed in Jeff's hand as DePalma hit the line.

Dust and thunder and chaos flooded that narrow road as we barreled out of town. Ahead, Dawson and Wilcox were fighting it out; to our right, Bob Whitney's Stutz was already dropping behind.

Dawson was dropping back now, as Wilcox surged ahead. Dawson's Marmon got bigger and bigger, as we bellowed into the first turn.

All the way around, we trailed him, riding his deck. Pulling out of it, Chip made his bid.

It was a daring challenge. The road here was just wide enough for two cars to pass. On either side, the ditch was abrupt. Joe moved over, to give us clearance, but Joe's foot didn't relax a bit. For two hundred yards, we paced it out in our Marmons along that treacherous, freshly graded strip. Then, slowly, Joe's thunder-wagon began to drop behind.

We were alone, in fourth place, as we slammed into the next curve, gaining steadily on the Marmon behind.

Ahead, there was nothing but dust. Somewhere in that dust were Nelson and DePalma and Wilcox. We might or might not catch them. Even if we didn't, we were doing all right—for apprentices.

The groups of spectators flashed by, like clumps of foliage, foliage with faces, as the Marmon roared down the longest stretch in the route. Most of the spectators preferred the curves. That's where the excitement was, that's where things happened—on the curves.

There was one of those coming up now, a high-crowned devil of a curve, hard in the center, soft at the edges, and sharp.

I took my eyes from the road, and watched Chip. With *anybody else* at the wheel, I wouldn't have had the nerve for that.

I saw that smile on his face, and I watched him change his grip on the wheel. Anticipation was plain, there, on that young face. And it wasn't *fearful*, it was *joyful* anticipation, if you follow me. *He loves it,* I thought, *he loves it all, including the danger.*

Money didn't motivate him, nor any quest for glory, nor even the competition. All these were part of it, of course, but it was the driving itself he truly relished, and the speed, the triumph of man over distance. It isn't something I am able to analyze correctly for you; it exists, it motivates them all, the good ones. There isn't enough money or glory to make the game worth the candle, unless you feel like that about it.

That's the way we felt, Chip and I.

He came into that curve under the brake of compression, and one third of the way through, he slammed the gun to her in a power spin. The rear end went wide, fighting for traction.

Right to the disaster-limit edge of that gully those screeching rear wheels lurched. And there they stopped their side-ward skid. Right on that rim, they found forward traction, and we cannoned into the stretch under full control.

That's Chip. That's my boy. And that's the game, always just one inch from immortality.

Our boiler was really singing now. The blob of dust ahead kept growing. It was Red Nelson, and from the black smoke that poured from his tail pipe, it was evident he was in trouble. We blasted by him as we hit the red-barn curve.

Third place, and we'd achieved it in the first circuit of the race.

In town, the route was solidly lined with spectators. Chip grinned and I waved, as they cheered. A little later, I waved again, to Mom, standing on the porch.

Ahead, we saw another blob of dust.

That Marmon went reaching for power, as Chip probed her. The blob grew closer. It was the National; it was Wilcox.

Two curves, and once again we were on the longest stretch in the run. The Marmon was all out, revving her top rev, and the music she made was a tribute to the hours we'd spent on her.

The National grew and grew and grew . . . .

It's no discredit to Howie to say he didn't have enough that day. He had enough, personally, but not enough under him. The Marmon swept by him before we hit the high-crowned curve.

Chip's accomplishment of it was a replica of the run before.

Roughly half the race was over, and we were in second place.

We should have been satisfied, I suppose. Our first race, and driving a rebuilt stock car. Our first race, and we were chasing DePalma home.

For that was the master's Simplex ahead. That was the juggernaut he drove to sixth place at Indianapolis the next year. It wouldn't have been any cause for shame, following DePalma home.

The Marmon was still souped to her roaring limit. And the Marmon was gaining . . . .

I couldn't believe it, at first. It must be an illusion, I thought. But the Simplex grew bigger and clearer, and then we were pressing him.

Our front hub was even with his rear, was up to the door, and the Simplex found another r.p.m. somewhere. It began to creep ahead, lengthen the lead.

Chip didn't cut the motor one bit, though the red barn was in sight, and the red-barn curve.

The Simplex climbed to a ten foot lead, and stayed

right there. I looked over at Chip, wondering when he was going to cut the power, but his squinting eyes were on the road ahead, trying to pierce the dust.

Pebbles rattled off our cowl, as the Simplex cut for the curve.

Chip made his bid, right then.

I remember gripping the side of the seat, and I remember how red and big that barn looked. I'll never forget the "bang" of that right rear tire, nor the lurching side-spin that followed it.

I don't recall my passage through the air, as the Marmon went over the bank. The crowd screamed, I remember—and the impact of my fall, and the darkness that followed . . . .

THREE

The faces came out of the dimness, and the voices were something other than the murmurings they had been.

It was a hospital room, I could see. Mom was at the foot of the bed, with a man who looked like a doctor.

Mom said, "You're going to be all right, Elmer. You've broken a leg, that's all." She tried a smile, but couldn't quite make it. Her eyes were wet.

Chip sat on a chair near the window, looking down at his hands.

I said, "We almost made it, boy. Don't look so glum." I grinned at him.

He looked up, out the window. He said, "They thought you had a—" He broke off, shaking his head. "Elmer, if I thought I'd—"

"Any spectators hurt?" I asked.

He shook his head.

"And you?" I asked him.

"I hit a hay stack."

"The car—"

He shrugged. "I don't know—"

The doctor said, "Young man, you've had a very

close call. I must insist that you get some rest. Tomorrow, you'll be more able to talk about these things."

"All right," I said, "but Chip, find out about the car, won't you? Find out how the motor is."

Mom came over to kiss me, as Chip said, "I'll bring you all the news, tomorrow." He still wouldn't look at me.

"A tire can go, any time," I said. "That's a part of the game. That's what makes it interesting."

"All right," he said, and smiled weakly. "I'll see you in the morning, if they'll let me, Elm."

The next day was Sunday, and he wouldn't be working.

It was a bad night. Some sort of reaction set in and my head ached for hours, matching the pain in my leg. I must have looked pretty bad when Chip arrived in the morning, for he was full of questions as to my condition.

I told him I was all right, and asked about the car.

"The frame's bent," he said, "but the motor's all right."

That was a relief. "The motor's the important thing," I told him. "We were going to cut that frame down, anyway."

He didn't say anything.

"Next season," I went on, "we'll have a real car, and we'll clean up."

He wasn't listening. He went over to look out the window. His back was to me, as he said, "Harold came to see me, last night."

I said nothing, waiting.

"He brought a message from my dad. Dad wants to set Harold and me up in the real estate business. He's got a lot of property we could subdivide and build on. Harold's all for it. He says there's big money to be made in it."

Again, I said nothing.

He turned to face me. "Well, what do you think?"

"You'll have to decide," I said. "I could use you in the shop, Chip. That factory's no place for you, that much I know. There's too much work at the shop for one man."

"I'd like that," he said. "I'd sure like that, Elm."

"But with your dad," I said, "your future is sure. Harold might be just what you need, a careful, steadying influence. With your ideas, and his caution, you might go a long, long way. We've got a banged-up Marmon and a garage business, now, that's all."

Again, he turned, to look out the window. "Do you really want me, Elm? Am I really worth my salt?"

"It's no charity," I answered. "I want you and need you."

"What have I ever brought you, but bad luck?" he said. "And aren't we foolish, maybe? Is it such a good business? Do we know how it will develop?"

"No," I said, "we don't have all the answers. But we know what we want. We know what we're suited for. The rest is a gamble, like anything worth while is a gamble."

He smiled then. "All right, Elm, it's a bargain. I'm—sorry I've been such a wet blanket lately, but —" He shrugged.

"You've enough reason to be serious," I agreed. Then I told him about the rest of my plans. For our attending the engineering school in town here this winter, and adding more space to the shop, and buying new tools.

When he left, he told me he was going back to pull the motor out of the Marmon. Mom, he said, was hiring a rig and would be in this afternoon. He seemed to be older and more grave when he left me.

Mom didn't come in a rig. Jean Calvin had come out to the house after learning about the accident. And she drove Mom over.

Jean seemed to bring the sunshine in with her. *If I hadn't seen Elaine first,* I thought, *I could fall in love with Jean.*

"Just think," Mom said, "she drives that big car like a man. Better than a lot of men."

"You didn't mean better than Chip, did you, Mom?" I asked her.

"I certainly did not." Then her voice softened. "Elmer, he seems different since he came back from the hospital this morning. He's going to be all right, isn't he?"

"He's going to be all right," I assured her. "Here I am with a broken leg and a possible concussion, and you worry about *him*."

"I know you're going to be all right," Mom said. "You're just like your father, and no bump in the head could hurt him." She smiled. "And besides, this young lady has been doing enough worrying about you for the two of us." She turned to Jean. "You can see for yourself he's as handsome as ever."

"I don't remember now whether Jean blushed or not, but I know I did. Maybe, Mom knew what I didn't. . . . Well, who can tell the road to take beforehand? Second guessing is too easy.

The Sunday before I left the hospital, Elaine came with Chip.

She looked faintly unhappy. I could guess that he'd told her about our plans. But she didn't look like she was considering herself out of Chip's plans, not yet.

Her blonde beauty seemed to brighten the whole

65

room. *Maybe,* I hoped, *Chip doesn't love her. Maybe, they're just old friends.* And maybe I was the Tsar of Russia.

I went home on Monday, a sharp, windy Monday that prophesied the winter to come. Jean brought me home, in her Reo. She did handle it like a man, with no nonsense, with forceful deftness.

She told me, "No matter what Chip's other friends think, I want you to know I'm on your side. You and Chip are doing exactly what you want to do and what you were designed to do."

"I wish Elaine felt that way," I said.

She nodded, her eyes on the road. "It would be better." She paused. "And—Elm, you *will* be careful, won't you?"

I promised I would.

That winter was a misery. The cold weather arrived with Thanksgiving and stayed for the season. The car business was nothing, the bicycle business less than that. But that wasn't what made it a bad winter. Chip and I figured out a quick change-over from buggy to sleigh, and had all the work we could handle. Between that, and going to school some afternoons and almost every evening, we didn't have a spare second. That's what made it a bad winter, because the Marmon went untouched, after Thanksgiving.

Two days before the new year, Chip learned that

his dad was in bed with pneumonia. He'd been running himself down, campaigning in behalf of party unity, and the weather had been too much for him.

Right after supper, on New Year's Eve, Harold Adams' big Mercedes drove into the yard. Judge Adams was worse, and the doctor thought it advisable Chip should come.

He looked scared and sick, when he left.

We'd had a little party planned, to welcome the new year, and Jean had promised to come out with Elaine. They came around eight, and I told them what had happened.

It wasn't much of a party, after that. At midnight, we toasted the new year, and then the cutter came to take the girls home. Mom went to bed.

I sat there, wide-awake and wondering in the cold parlor, until dawn when Chip came.

The crisis was over, he told me, and the Judge was resting well. He slumped down on the horse-hair sofa. "Harold says I'll kill Dad, if I don't change," Chip said quietly. "Harold says I'm not only ruining my dad's health, I'm spoiling my chances and his own for a respectable future."

I said, "A young man as *intelligent* and *sensible* as Harold shouldn't need any help with his future."

"A sensible man wouldn't turn his back on a quarter of a million dollars, either," Chip said.

I'd never realized they were *that* rich. "No," I agreed, "he wouldn't. A man would need to be a blind fool to turn his back on that kind of money."

"That's what I am," Chip said, "a blind fool. And that's what I intend to remain."

"In that case," I said, "you're in good company."

Chip grinned weakly, and shook his head. "We haven't heard the last from dear Cousin Harold, you can bet on that. He's determined that I don't spoil *his* chances with this foolishness. We'll hear from him again, somehow."

"He scares me to death," I scoffed. "I hope he doesn't strike me."

"You don't know him," Chip said. "He's a very, very clever lad."

"I'll try not to let it disturb my dreams," I said. "I think we could both stand some sleep, don't you?"

He nodded, and rose. He put a hand on my arm. "And Elm—thanks for waiting up. I sure was glad to see— Well, thanks."

We went up to bed.

We studied and worked, and planned for the summer. It wasn't only engineering and mechanics we studied. Chip got interested in Freud, who was causing such a stir, and he got me interested, too. I guess Chip was trying to find something that would help him understand his dad.

Jean had me reading some Shaw, too, and I thought he was a pretty smart man, for an Irishman. I'm no scholar or historian, but both Shaw and Freud must have influenced the change that was coming over the country at that time. I guess you could include Irving Berlin in that, too, and maybe Henry Ford, and even the turkey trot that was to cause so much fuss in the press later.

In January, an airplane took off from and alighted on water for the first time in history. In January, President Taft sent a congratulatory message to Emperor William of Germany on achieving his fifty-second birthday. Mr. Taft expressed the good will that we bore for the Emperor's country.

In January, Chip was working on some plans for a motor he had in mind, and I was helping him. Just for the sport of it, not with any definite project in mind. It was a part of our schooling.

The thaw came in March, late in March. Winter left as abruptly as it had arrived. Our business was growing; the showing we had made in the road race, before the tire blew, had brought us to the attention of all the town's younger motorists. We hired a student from the school we were attending, and enlarged the shop.

In April, Jim Masker came to work for us. Jim had a small foundry in town, but it wasn't doing very well, and he was handy mechanically. We were glad to have him. He was older; he would be a good man to leave in the shop when we went on the road again.

Jim closed his foundry, but didn't sell it. He had some offers, I know, but he wouldn't sell. I couldn't understand that, at the time, because he seemed to be intending to stay on with us.

In April, spring came for sure. That was the month we finally went to work on the Marmon. Chip came to life again.

How we worked that spring! We cut the old frame down, and slung it even lower between the new wire wheels. We upped the compression to a point where we feared we might not get a fuel to handle it. We geared her way up, figuring to use our faster second for the turns. We added a reserve gas tank, with a cut-in, a little idea of Chip's whereby we could cut in the reserve from one tank to the other. That way, we'd need pressure in only one tank, we'd need only one pump.

Outside, the days got more golden and the sun climbed higher in the sky, while we stayed in that dim garage, working. Even Jim Masker caught the fever and pitched in to help us with the Marmon.

One day, right after lunch, Elaine and Jean drove out in the Reo. They thought it was too fine a day to waste at work, and an ideal day for a picnic.

There was no denying them, nor the day, and Chip and I went in to scrub up.

We drove all the way out to park at Swan Lake. There were benches under the trees, and canoes for hire.

A canoe is made for two people, at the most, we decided. Elaine and Chip took one, Jean and I another.

What Chip and Elaine talked about, I didn't find out until later. Jean and I talked about Shaw and Teddy Roosevelt and Irving Berlin—and the gasoline engine Chip and I were working on with Jim Masker. Jim was going to cast the block, once we decided definitely on the design.

"Your plans go further than that, don't they?" she guessed. "You're not going to stop with a motor."

"Our plans go further than that," I admitted. "But not our purses."

"What are you going to call your automobile?" she asked.

"We haven't decided," I said, and smiled a little sheepishly. "Do you think it's—silly, Jean?"

"I think it's wonderful," she answered, and I knew she meant it.

And when we all met again, for the basket supper the girls had brought, Elaine made her announcement. She and Chip were engaged.

It was no surprise to me, and no shock. I was

happy for both of them. If I'd had a little more sense, I'd have known why, right then. But I didn't realize that until later.

Elaine said, "Chip's going to quit racing, too, after this season, aren't you, Chip?"

"I didn't promise that," he said. "I only admitted there was a possibility I might." He looked at me.

I knew what the possibility was and it was an uncertain possibility. Elaine, I felt sure, was in for a disappointment. Unless we had a very, very lucky year.

We took the Marmon out for a road test three days later. She was still a road-hugging, power-packed sweetheart. She took those unbanked curves like a train on a track, and just ate the stretches.

We'd shortened the wheel base, to make her adaptable to track racing. We were ready for anything, now.

When we came back to the garage, we had a three man huddle with Jim Masker. Jim was all set to cast the block of our new motor, and it was the finance-raising strategy that concerned us now.

We talked about Louis Chevrolet who had signed a paper, that year, that should have made him eventually one of the richest men in the world. His new Chevrolet, designed for W. C. Durant included the first counterbalanced crankshaft, the first gear shift lever in the middle of the floor. He'd tried to get skirts on the fenders, too, but nobody was prepared to make them.

Louis Chevrolet was about to become one of the truly big men in the automobile game. He always will be, but not, as it developed, from a financial standpoint.

"And how did he get where he is?" Chip asked.

We knew the answer to that. Chevrolet had first attracted attention to his abilities as a racing driver and designer. There was money—promotional money—for names and ability, particularly in a field as venturesome and sporting as the automobile business.

I said, "But we've got to hit the big ones. We've got to race against the name drivers—and win."

We laid out the schedule. The Grand American, outside of Chicago, Indianapolis, and some others. We would wind up with the big one, the Worthington Cup, the rockiest, roughest test for man and motors that had ever been devised. That would be in September.

We had been making money, but we'd spent plenty, in enlarging the shop to a garage, in rebuilding the Marmon. And we'd spend more on the road, shipping the car and ourselves from race to race. We could only hope that the men we'd hired could handle the business without us.

"Maybe I'd better stay back here," I suggested.

"You're going to drive half of them," Chip said. "You know you couldn't stay behind."

"I can't drive any of them," I lied. "My leg isn't right yet." My ego has never had a stunted growth, but I always knew who the driver was in *that* combination.

We decided, finally, that we'd both go up to Palmyra, for the fifty mile melee they were staging, and decide about the others afterward.

It was at Palmyra that we ran into J. Alexander Sloan, and his boys. The Triple-A knows all about Alec. He caused them enough trouble from a promotional standpoint for them to remember him to this day. He managed Barney Oldfield, and handled, in his time, Tommy Milton, Eddie Hearne, Leon Duray, Sig Haugdahl, and plenty of others.

Alec loved the game and he was one of the great promoters of all time. He put the color into automobile racing. Our debt to him will never be repaid.

But the May day we met him at Palmyra, the first time we had occasion to deal with this man in the loud suit, we didn't have history's viewpoint.

For Sloan had a *team,* and on a one mile horse track, a team is about all you need for victory. Two men to do the boxing, and one man to do the winning.

Alec knew what the public wanted. What it

wanted was a "hippodrome finish." That meant a seesaw all the way to the last stretch, and then three or four cars fighting it out hub and hub to the checkered flag. The crowd would tear up the seats, for one of those. Alec was a great believer in democracy. Democracy, to him, meant giving the people just what they wanted.

At Palmyra, in addition to Sloan, there was a man who had made a name for himself as a bicycle racer and motor bike racer, but who will be best remembered for his exploits behind the wheel of his "Peerless Green Dragon," or the "Golden Egg"—Henry Ford's old "999"—which traveled two miles a minute. The man who made the Blitzen Benz famous in this country. The man with the cigar—Barney Oldfield.

We were in the pits. It was a fine May morning, and the sweet smell of burning oil perfumed the quiet air. Chip was putting on his goggles, getting ready for a trial run.

In the next pit, Joe Crider was talking to the manager of his team. It was Sloan. He finished with Joe, and walked over to our pit.

"Don't think I know you boys," he said, and introduced himself.

"We're new to the game," I said. "My name is Elmer Ryan, and this is Chip Adams." We shook hands all around.

Sloan was looking at the Marmon. "That's a lot of car."

We agreed it was.

"New to the game, huh?"

We just nodded.

He looked thoughtful. Finally, he said, "Boys, you're in fast company. Let me give you a word of advice."

We waited respectfully.

"You've got a fast car, and you're both young. You've got a future ahead of you. Don't spoil it. Do your best, but never force yourself or your machine beyond that limit. Take defeat with silence and victory with modesty. It's a rough, tough game, and you can't win them all."

It was good advice, and honestly meant. But it seemed to us then he was preparing our minds for inevitable defeat in the fifty miler. We'd heard about his team.

Chip said, "We came here to win, Mr. Sloan. We've got the car, and I think we can do it."

"Of course," Sloan said, "of course." He nodded. "It should be an interesting race." He went back to Crider's pit.

Crider and his mechanic came over to help me push the Marmon to a start. As we walked back, Crider said, "If that buggy is what she looks like, yours is the number one car to watch."

The music of her drifted back from the south turn. "She's a sweetheart," I said, "but we've got something on the drafting board that's better."

I was young and hopeful and impressed by those around me. I was trying to do a little impressing myself.

Crider said, "You'll have to go some to beat that Marmon motor."

I didn't tell him that wasn't our intention. I didn't want him to know we were thinking of a car for the middle classes. The company was too rich for talk like that. I said, "That's the purpose of engineering, to go beyond the present."

He sort of stared at me, and went back to his pit. I don't blame him. I was young, I repeat. I have no other alibi.

Chip made the Marmon talk. That boy. . . . How all that talent and nerve and skill can be wrapped up in a hundred and fifty pounds of human is something I'll never understand. The tracks and roads of that day were unbanked or poorly banked, the cars heavy. It was all wrist and nerve, but Chip came through.

He took a couple of easy, warm-up laps and then threw away the anchor. The roar of that big motor seemed to shake the ground, as he arrowed past the pits. They were all watching from the pits.

Into the south he thundered, and the fan of dirt

he threw was like an avalanche as the wheels fought for traction. I held my breath. All the way around the south turn, I held my breath. He made it.

The north, he almost didn't make. The Marmon started to climb the bank the moment he hit the curve. She was sluing sideways, and I worried about those new wheels, those untried wire wheels. If one of them crumpled. . . .

But they weren't as frail as they looked, and one of our theories was confirmed. The wheels held. And, just as it seemed timber would surely fly, Chip's wrists held, too. He stopped the skid, right next to the fence, and gunned down-track, under control.

I expelled my breath.

When he came back to the pits, I said, "Nice wheeling. But maybe a little too fast for this track, don't you think?"

"I was showing off," he admitted. "I wanted them —to know—"

"Sure," I said. "Well, they know, now."

"Those wheels are all right," Chip said. "They make the car hang better, too. And they'll sure save time on a tire change."

I planned to stay in the pits, for this one. We hired another mechanic just for the race, and he and I would be waiting in the pits, with a couple of spare wheels with mounted tires. Tires weren't

78

what they are now. Fifty miles of rough dirt raised hob with them, at racing speeds.

We had the car, we had the wheels, we had Chip Adams. The rest, as they say, was in the lap of the gods.

They used qualifying trials for the starting positions, and Chip was a little more careful this time. He qualified for the inside spot in the third row.

Flanking him, in the Peerless, was Barney Oldfield.

It was a gloomy afternoon, I remember, with the threat of rain, but that didn't stop the fans. The grandstand was overflowing, and the infield jammed with standing customers. It was Barney's name that had brought them; most of the other giants weren't taking a chance on this one, so close to Indianapolis time.

The starter went down the rows, checking them all; the mechanics and pit monkeys stood by, to start the motors.

Then it came, the rumble of all those big motors coming to life, the last check by the starter, as he waved them around for the flying start. Fifty miles of speed on a flat track, fifty miles of legalized murder. I was almost glad I wasn't riding along, almost. . . .

Around—at a rising pace, jockeying to maintain position, to find a favorable position for the starting challenge. Around—with the dust rising like a swarm of insects, adding to the day's gloominess. Into the north turn swiftly, and out of it at a steadily increasing gait. In the starter's hand, the green flag was high.

The roar and the flame-tipped tail pipes, as the green flag dropped. For the first time, this track which had known only the drumming of horses' feet felt the full shuddering impact of an automobile race. I thought I could feel it tremble.

It was Joe Crider, right from the jump-off. Joe's Stutz seemed to leap at the drop of the flag, and Joe broadsided into the first turn all alone. His flanking man, Earl Cooper, trailed him by fifteen feet into the bend.

Crider, Cooper, Nelson, Lutz—those were the first four. Some fifty yards behind Crider, Chip and Barney fought for the rail, and for the privilege of holding down fifth place.

Then Barney's green job moved ahead, and then past Lutz, as they came down grandstand alley for the first time. The stands were up, and shouting.

It was much too fast a first lap for a fifty mile grind, much too fast. Dust flew back like a tidal wave as they roared by.

In the backstretch, Lutz was finished. His rebuilt Pope-Hartford was faltering, spitting and coughing. He came limping into the pits, next time around.

Chip rode fifth. And from his four spot, Barney made his bid.

He got past Red Nelson. But ahead, Crider and Cooper were waging a bitter two-man war of their own, and there simply wasn't room to get by, not on that track.

For ten laps, while the dust thickened, while the dirt piled up near the outer rail, the three of them fought it out. On the fourteenth lap, Barney was forced to drop behind.

In the backstretch, Chip sneaked past Red Nelson and edged up on Barney's Peerless. He found a spot about fifty feet behind, and there he stayed, waiting for his chance.

The laps went on. In the heavy, humid air the smell of dust and oil blanketed the area, hugged the ground. Crider, Cooper, Barney and Chip, into the twenty-fifth lap.

Into the thirtieth, and it looked like a merry-go-round, now, that wasn't ever going to change. Chip, I thought, was creeping up a little, but not much, not enough for anyone else to notice.

Then, coming into the backstretch, the Marmon seemed to take wings. Chip was on Barney's deck, was even with his rear wheels, was hub and hub, in as short a time as it takes to say it. They paced it out into the north turn, and were lost then in the haze of dust.

Chip came out leading by ten feet!

How he did it, I'll never know, but that's the way it was. The Marmon was screaming as they see-sawed past the pits. Into the south, now, their motors snarling. Both cars rode high on the bank, and disappeared into the dust.

I watched the skyline for the sign of flying timber and listened for the crash that was certainly coming.

Then, on the far end of the turn, I saw the Marmon's big hood, I saw the entire Marmon and twenty feet of open space before the snout of the Peerless came surging out.

My boy Chip was now holding down the three spot.

But the Green Dragon lost not a foot in the next three laps. And slowly, the pair of them were crawling up on the leader. Crider and Cooper rode one-two, but each in the speed groove. There was room to go by, now.

Thirty-eight laps, thirty-nine—I watched Chip's right rear tire, each time he blasted by, looking for that first sign of fraying, of imminent disaster. The tires held.

On the forty-second lap, Chip made his bid for the lead. Cooper chose that moment to make a bid of his own. He swung out, as Chip came closer.

It was the story of the early race repeating itself.

There wasn't room, not for three cars abreast on those turns. In the stretches, the Marmon didn't have it; the stretches were too short. It wasn't just a motor that would decide this. It was courage, or a lack of sense, whichever you want to call it.

The Green Dragon came up to join the fun.

Four cars, now, riding too close for sanity, riding each other's nerves, sending the dusty crowd into a delirium. It was no place for a kid, but the kid was doing all right.

Forty-five laps, forty-six. . . . It looked like it would be a hippodrome finish. Chip still claims that's what was planned, though he isn't bitter about it any more. What Chip didn't realize and what I couldn't drive home to him for a long time was that Cooper was a free-lance entry, just as we were. And Cooper was the key.

It was Cooper who swung out to block Chip's path. And though Crider did his level best to shake him, though Crider had his thunder-wagon right down to the floor, Cooper stuck to him like a brother. It was straight driving, all the way. I was sure of it, then; I know it, now.

Forty-seven laps, forty-eight. . . .

Everybody in the stands was on his feet. Everybody was hoarse and weak and dusty, as the four-car parlay streaked by. The laggards had coasted into the pits; they wanted no part of this.

Forty-nine laps. . . .

Then, in the backstretch, something happened. I didn't hear Cooper's tire go, but I saw his car start to slide, as Chip tried to edge by.

I saw Barney cut low, and get by. I saw him, in a very neat display of power application, cut wide in the next split-second, and steal the lead from Crider.

Cooper's job seemed to be drifting, and then it swung in a complete arc. Chip had gone for the brakes, but not in time. The front of Cooper's whirling iron smashed into the left front wheel of the Marmon. The Marmon went into a slide of its own, as the stands screamed, as Barney came out of the north turn, all alone, bearing down on the checkered flag.

I started to run through the infield.

FOUR

The Marmon was up against the fence, just resting there, facing the wrong way. Chip, thank God, was all right. He had climbed from the car, and was outside the fence. Cooper was all right, too.

Or rather, he was, until Chip landed that fist right on his nose.

I watched in amazement, as the spectators from that side of the track stepped between them, Chip fighting like a young wildcat. When the track was clear, I went over to calm him down.

Cooper went to get help for his car, and the crowd began to disperse. I guided Chip over toward the Marmon.

"You saw what happened," he said. "He and Crider were blocking the track, so Oldfield could come through for one of those last lap finishes."

"I don't believe it," I said. "I don't even think Cooper works for the team. He just didn't have enough stuff to get by Crider, and Crider didn't have enough to shake him."

There wasn't much wrong with the Marmon. That ridge of soft dirt at the edge of the track had acted as a brake, this time, and slowed the car to a halt short of the fence. The left front wheel was about twenty yards up the track.

Chip said, "The spindle's broken."

"We were lucky, if that's all," I answered.

"We're lucky," Chip said, "*if* we can get another spindle."

We had changed the spindles when we'd gone over from disc to wire wheels. It was a new firm, and I wasn't sure how well stocked they were on parts.

Then Cooper came over to where we stood. "You've got a poke in the nose coming, son," he said. "I always repay my debts."

"Beat it," I said. "Chip made a mistake. He thought you were trying to pull something."

Chip said, "I don't need any help, Elm, not with him."

Cooper took a threatening step forward, and Chip swung again. Only, this time, Chip caught him on the chin.

Cooper went down, and out!

I couldn't help it, then; I started to laugh. Jack Cooper was broad and bulky; I'd worried about him a little, myself. And at that moment, I thought of Mom saying, "—*that poor, little Chip.*"

Chip and I went over to get a dolly, so we could push the Marmon into the pits. But we didn't need it. There was a tow truck there, complete with hoist.

88

I knew it belonged to Alec Sloan, but Chip didn't, so I told the driver what we wanted, and slipped him a bill.

Chip and I went over to the hotel, to wash up. We would have to put some kind of wheel or spindle on the Marmon before we could load it on a train. But neither of us felt much like tackling it right now.

Chip said, "Oldfield won, didn't he?" We were in our room.

I nodded.

"I'll beat him," Chip said. "Some day, I'll beat him."

"He beat you fair and square," I said. "Barney doesn't need any help from anybody."

"All right," Chip answered. "All right. But I'll beat him, some day, and it'll be fair and square, too. You can put that in your book." He sat on the big brass bed and started to take off his shoes. "I should have beat him today."

"Don't be a poor loser," I said. "Let's forget this one. Let's think about the next one."

"We needed this one," he said. "We need them all."

There was a knock at the door, and I went to open it. It was Sloan. There was another man with him, a well-dressed man, a bit too well-dressed.

"Come in, gentlemen," I said.

I saw Chip stiffen and sit more erectly on the bed.

Sloan said, "Mr. Ryan, Mr. Adams, this is Mr. Ellington Duffy."

I shook hands with Mr. Duffy, but Chip just nodded.

Sloan frowned at Chip's rudeness. Then he said, "Joe Crider's told me a little about you boys, and I'm sure Mr. Duffy would be interested in you. I thought we could have a little supper together, this evening, and—"

"We'll be busy," Chip said.

Sloan looked at Chip, and his eyes were thoughtful. "Young man," he said evenly, "I came here to do both of you lads a favor. Mr. Duffy is interested in up-and-coming young men who are out to make a name for themselves. You seem like a likely pair, to me—"

Chip said, "We're not interested. Good-by, Mr. Sloan."

I should have said something, then, I know, because Chip was being unreasonable. I should have tried to bring him around. But this Ellington Duffy didn't look like much to me, either. I just looked at Sloan, and shrugged.

After they'd left, I went to the window. I saw them climb into a Locomobile. It wasn't Sloan's, I knew. I said to Chip, "I think we made a mistake. It wouldn't cost anything to listen."

"Does Duffy look like a banker to you?" Chip asked. "He's another promoter, and he's trying to build a racing team, I'll bet. He surely didn't look like money to me."

"He didn't look like a banker," I admitted, "or a man with money. But then, he didn't look like a man who'd be driving a Locomobile, either."

"Locomobile—?" Chip said, and came to the window.

"Locomobile," he said again, with awe, as the big car drove away. He was still staring out the window when I went down the hall to take a bath.

We managed to get a makeshift wheel on the Marmon, and load her, next morning. It was while I was putting the wheel into the car that I noticed something peculiar.

I showed the spindle to Chip. "What would you say was wrong with that?"

He stared at it, and then at me. "It's been heated. It wasn't lubricated right, and the friction burned it up. It wasn't the bump that broke it."

"Probably not," I said, and bent to look at the exposed wheel bearings. "It was never packed," I said.

"Didn't you—"

I shook my head. "Jim Masker packed that wheel."

"Lordy—" Chip said.

91

"We won't say anything to him," I suggested. "It'll only make him feel bad. You're alive. After this, we'll check everything ourselves."

He nodded. "Jim doesn't realize the speed we travel at. He's new to this business."

Chip didn't have anything to say on the trip home.

Jim met the train at the station. His eyes questioned us. "How'd you do?" he said.

"I had trouble," Chip told him. "I was doing all right until then."

Jim looked startled. "*You* drove? I thought Elmer was going to drive."

"Not me," I said. "Chip's the driver. Chip's the boy who'll have to bring home the bacon." I said nothing about the spindle.

We could either put the old disc wheels back on, or wait for the spindle we'd ordered. We agreed it would be better to wait for the spindle. The garage was behind in its work and we could get that cleaned up before the spindle came.

We worked early and late. As the only garage in town with any decent equipment, we got all the business and we had to turn most of it down. We were so busy, we lost track of time.

The spindle came, finally, just one day after the entries closed for Indianapolis.

That hit us hard, despite the fact we were still way behind in our work and that the trip would have put us even farther behind. We had wanted to race in the first "500." We started work even earlier and stopped later. Gradually, we got caught up. And gradually, we forgot about Indianapolis.

Early in June, we had the Marmon ready again. I had added a fine screen to the front of the radiator, a little trick I'd picked up at Palmyra. On those dirt tracks, the dust packed the radiator core, causing the engine to boil over. The screen, I thought, would protect against that and against any flying pebble that might be shot back by the wheels of the car ahead.

As it happened, I didn't have to worry too much about the car ahead, not in the next grind, anyway. That was the fifty miler at St. Paul.

I didn't want to go along for that one. I can't say why, but I felt my place was at the garage, while things were humming as they were. Chip couldn't see it.

"We've got Jim, and the boy, here," he argued, "and we can get another from the school to help. You're not forgetting the plans we made, are you, Elm? You're not thinking this garage business is the big thing?"

"It'll support us, while we're trying for the big thing," I said. "The Wrights are keeping their bicycle business, even though airplanes are *their* big thing."

"But when they go to Kitty Hawk," Chip pointed out, "they *both* go. I—need you, at St. Paul, Elm. I know who the engineer is, in this combination."

That did it. I went to St. Paul. I realized, later, why I hated so to leave the garage. I was afraid that Jim wasn't quite the mechanic we needed as boss of the shop. But just because he had neglected the Marmon's wheel bearing, I told myself, it wouldn't necessarily follow that he was lax in all his work. And besides, I had wanted to go to St. Paul.

It should have been cold up there, early in June. But it wasn't. It was fairly cool, with just enough dampness to improve carburetion, but not cold. And Chip was hotter than an exhaust valve.

The screen may have protected the radiator from some dust; I don't remember now. But I didn't need to worry about flying pebbles, nor the car ahead. Chip saw to that.

The competition wasn't too rugged at St. Paul, with one exception. The exception was Ray Harroun. Ray had been Triple-A champ the year before, and he'd won the big one at Indianapolis less than a month before. He had his Marmon along, and it was a dilly.

It's all there, in the records, and no one can take it away from Ray. His place in racing history is assured. Chip was just on, that's all. When Chip

Adams is on, *nobody* is going to make him look bad.

He won the pole in the time trials, and was never headed. He set a new one-lap record, a new ten-lap record and a new record for the half century. He had the stands up and roaring, time and again. Ray saw to it that he had some competition and Ray rode his tail every mile of the way. Ray was still riding his tail right down to the checkered flag.

In the pits, as the crowd swarmed out to congratulate him, Chip looked as cocky as though the race had yet to be run. It was like a stimulating narcotic to him, winning against that kind of competition. He loved it.

When the crowd had gone and we were getting the car cleaned up, he said, "That's only the first one, Elm. I can't lose, the way I feel now. With this car in the shape she is, and the way I feel, I *can't* lose."

"Easy, boy," I cautioned him. "Lot of miles ahead of us."

"You'll see," he said.

At Springfield, I saw. It certainly looked as though he'd spoken the truth. He led all the way, setting a new track record. He was unbeatable, that afternoon, again. I mean, in that field, he was unbeatable. None of the giants were in that field.

At the Cayuga Fairgrounds, I was afraid it was

95

going to be a different story. DePalma was there, for one. Some others were there, too, but you never knew they existed, after the race started.

It was Chip and DePalma. It was a dogfight, right from the jump-off, a two-car duel, a seesaw battle that gave the fans no rest. It gave me enough heart-stopping excitement to last me the rest of my life.

I was in the pits, for that one, and the pits never looked so sweet as they did that day.

I stood there, watching them make a bumpy, dangerous mess of that track, watching one ride the other's deck into turn after turn, crowding their luck, first one in the lead, then the other. I saw them rub hubs, and pull clear. I saw both of them slide so high on the north turn, I *knew* they'd both go through the timber. But they didn't.

And in the hot haze of dust and smoke and excitement, I saw Ralph kick his thunder-wagon home in front by a scant five feet as the flag dropped. Chip had no kick on that last leg of the lap.

In the pit, he looked unhappy. He sat there, staring up the track, saying nothing.

"You can't win 'em all," I said.

"No," he admitted, not looking at me. "And especially in the big leagues." He looked at me, now. "That was as fast and as good a race as I ran at Springfield or St. Paul, Elm. And it wasn't enough."

"Not today, it wasn't," I admitted. "You were up

against one of the best in the world today, Chip."

"I know it," he said. "I'm beginning to realize it. And the best is something different, isn't it? It might not be my league."

"You've been beaten by Oldfield," I said, "and by DePalma. There's no shame in that. You haven't beaten either of them. You may never beat them. But you're new to this game, and you gave Ralph a run for his money, right down to the flag. What more do you expect, your first year?"

"I don't know," he said. "All I know is, I had the car, I had the breaks, and I didn't win."

I put a hand on his shoulder. "The Grand National's coming up, Chip. Lots of races are coming up."

"All right," he said, and he grinned. "We'll see—"

Riding back home again, on the train, we talked about our new motor. We didn't mention the race.

A model had been cast, and it was all we'd hoped it would be. The garage was making money, but there was never going to be enough money in the business to finance that motor, and the car we hoped to build around it. The purses we had won didn't quite meet the racing expenses, so far. But the purses weren't our big concern. What we wanted and needed was prestige, the kind of prestige that came from being a top man in the field.

That kind of prestige would attract promoters

with *big money*. Big money was the only kind that could finance our proposed car. The custom-built cars made in small shops were a thing of the past, now. Mass production was the trend, and mass production needed large-scale financing. Perhaps, though, racing wasn't the right road to take. Perhaps, it was a little too rocky for a couple of beginners with an idea, for a driver with only four races behind him. I couldn't see any other road, though, not for me. And not for Chip.

Back at the shop, Jim told us that business had fallen off, a little. The two of them were able to handle it adequately. He asked us how we had done.

"We did all right," I said. Chip said nothing. I told Jim about St. Paul and Springfield.

"Tell him about Cayuga," Chip said. "Tell him about DePalma."

"DePalma beat us," I said.

"Again," Chip added.

Jim said, "You kids are backing the wrong horse. There's no future in that game. You're wasting your talents."

"It's not the money we're after," I told him. "It's the fame that comes with winning."

"You've got to beat the big boys to get any publicity," Jim pointed out. "And beating the big boys at their own game is something to do."

"Some day," I answered, "you come out and watch Chip drive. Maybe you'll change your mind."

He never came out. Whether he changed his mind, or not, I'm in no position to say.

We really worked that Marmon over for the next one. The next one was the Grand American Road Race—and I'd be riding again.

It was a tricky route, with some hairpin curves, but the road was wide and well graded, the ditches shallow. Howie Wilcox was there. He said it was made for him, that race, and the rest of us could go home.

Howie still had his four-cylinder National, and he hadn't done so well at Indianapolis. But Indianapolis wasn't a road race, and there was a good chance his jesting words would come true now. He was a very able man, on the road.

Howie's side-kick, Joe Dawson, was, there, too. Joe's National had a little less displacement than Wilcox's, but it was big enough to win the 500 the next year. That was the year DePalma was leading by twenty miles when his motor conked out. Ralph pushed it across the finish line, but he was disqualified.

DePalma was there, with his new Mercedes. He wasn't in the Mercedes the day we first ran into him, though. He had one foot on the running board of a big Locomobile, and he was talking to a man in the back seat.

The man was Ellington Duffy.

"Ralph's a lot more democratic than we are, it looks like," I said.

"All right," said Chip, "so I was a sap." I didn't argue with him.

Ralph waved and we waved back. Ellington Duffy didn't wave, so we couldn't wave back at him. Duffy sat in the softly upholstered rear seat of his Locomobile, smoking a big cigar, and ignoring us. I can't say that I blame him.

DePalma, Dawson, Wilcox—those were three of them, and some others I've forgotten now, good boys, every one. They were out to win, and if they couldn't, to make it hot for the winner. Out to try, at any rate, this torrid July day, and with the equipment to make their efforts formidable.

Good boys, I repeat, every one of them. But nothing to make you overlook Chip Adams, in our Marmon. Nothing that would make a good bet, from any angle. I should say something about my own small part—about the hours I had put into that motor, the way I'd worked her down to the finest edge she'd ever had, about the skinned knuckles and throbbing head it had cost me. You'll look a long time before you see any ribbons for mechanics.

But I was a part of it. I knew the giants, and I'm proud of the memory.

It seemed like everybody led the race, for a while. DePalma had the early lead, and then Wilcox took it away. Some youngster by the name of Cole caught Howie on the second hairpin, when Howie slued wide. The two of them fought it out for five miles. Then Dawson got into it.

All of this I read later. We were back in fifth place, making no bid for the entire first half of the race. The Marmon was at its peak. Chip knew that. He wasn't afraid to lay back, not in a grind as tough as this, not with that Marmon perking like she was.

I thought he was cutting it pretty fine, but I'd been wrong before on my timing. I had no reason to doubt his sense of pace. We rode along at a brisk clip, biding our time, through the dust and the heat, past the solidly lined spectators, waiting, waiting, waiting. . . .

It must have been exactly at the halfway mark that Chip put the spurs to the Marmon. I gripped the edge of my seat, and hung on.

There was one curve I knew we couldn't make, not at the speed we had reached. But we did. We passed Cole, right after that curve. We passed Wilcox and Dawson, too, but not without a battle.

Ahead, way, way ahead we could make out the

funnel of dust that must be DePalma. The road was straight here, and Chip was smiling that smile. *Hang on, Elmer,* I told myself, *you ain't seen nothing yet.*

The motor roar was something I can't describe, the wind was a solid, howling wall.

But the funnel of dust grew bigger and bigger, until we could recognize the Mercedes.

There was no curve ahead. This was the straightaway stretch to home, to the checkered flag. No skill involved from here in, only nerve, and the condition of the motor.

The Mercedes was wide open, the Marmon was wide open, and anything could happen. The Marmon was gaining.

Ralph's mechanic turned around and saw us, and the Mercedes edged over, to give us room. We pulled even, not three hundred yards from the checkered flag.

We pulled even, and that's all. It was nose and nose for two hundred of those three hundred yards, neither car gaining an inch. Ralph must have found an extra rev somewhere in that Mercedes.

I closed my eyes, and tried to close my ears against the racket. I opened my eyes, and we had a two foot lead—about a one skinned knuckle lead.

And that's what we beat Ralph DePalma by, two

feet, in the Grand American Road Race, outside of Chicago, in the hot July of 1911.

I don't think I'll ever forget that. I guess Ralph won't, either. Chip and I sat in the Marmon, while they congratulated us, while they gave us the cup and the check. We sat there and grinned, and grinned and grinned until our faces got tired.

At the hotel, that night, I asked Chip, "Still think you're not big enough for those boys?"

"It was straight stuff," Chip said. "It was a test of motors, and we had the motor. You know that, Elm."

"Of course I know it," I agreed. "I just wanted to hear you admit it."

Back at the garage, business was only fair. The other shops, Jim explained, were catching up to us so far as equipment went. We'd do well, he thought, to plow a little of our profits back into the business. We needed more tools. We needed a new tow truck, with a hoist, and more windows in the garage.

"And we'll need lower gearing, in this Marmon, for the Worthington cup," Chip said. "That's no level run, the Worthington."

Jim shook his head. "You kids make me sick. You won a big race, and now you'll never give this shop the attention it needs. How can you leave a business like this, and go chasing rainbows?"

We had all kinds of answers for that, Chip and I. But the *reason* was something else, and how can a man explain that? How can a man explain the magic of beating DePalma?

Jim said, "With a little active promotion, this stop would really pay. With new equipment, and a little pushing—"

I said, "We don't want to gear that Marmon any differently until after that century run at Palmyra. We'll have time after that."

Jim walked away, muttering something, and Chip winked at me. We didn't really expect any sane people to understand us.

For the hundred miler, we'd need both tanks, the regular and the reserve. I planned to bring the gas from the garage; I wasn't too sure of the gas I could get any place else, *including* a race track. I knew ours was good.

Chip went to see Elaine, the night before we left. I couldn't visit Jean. She was in Canada for the summer.

I was still up, reading, when Chip came home. He looked like the last rose of summer.

"You've been quarreling," I said.

He nodded. "As usual. She claims now that I promised I'd quit at the end of this season."

"Maybe we can," I said.

"I'm not quitting," Chip said, "until my name's worth money, enough money to back that motor."

I reflected, as he went up to bed, that if he hadn't been such a headstrong lad, his name would have been worth about a quarter of a million dollars some time ago.

It was at Palmyra that we had first met J. Ellington Duffy. And his Locomobile was again very much in evidence as we pulled the Marmon into the pits next day.

Duffy, himself, was over near the Sloan pits, talking to Crider. If he was aware of our existence, he didn't show it.

Duffy left, after a while, and Crider came over to our pits. He and I shook hands. Chip pretended to be busy with the motor.

Crider said, "You boys have gone a long way since I last saw you. I see you won the Grand American."

"Chip did," I said. "Chip and the Marmon."

Crider winked at me. "I see his disposition hasn't improved any. I thought I was doing you boys a favor when I told Mr. Duffy about that motor of yours. But I guess not, the way your friend treated him."

Chip looked up, now. He said nothing, just stared at Crider. I remembered it was at this track that Chip had swung on Cooper. I said quickly, "I guess we all make mistakes. This Duffy a—pretty big man?"

"A *big* man?" Crider's laugh was scornful. "You mean you've never heard of the Duffy Wagons?"

Duffy Wagons . . . I guess everybody had heard of them. Studebaker Wagons, and Duffy Wagons—they did the bulk of America's transportation business. I looked at Chip. He didn't look quite so belligerent, now.

I said, "You—told him about our motor? You mean, the motor I told you about—the—" I took a deep breath. "I thought Duffy wanted to see us about a racing team."

"Heck, no," Crider said. "Mr. Duffy's beginning to suspect that the horse isn't the complete answer to the transportation game. He's thinking of going into the automobile business."

"But Sloan was with him," I protested. "Sloan isn't interested in—"

"Alec Sloan," Crider said, "is one good guy, in spite of what your hotheaded friend over there might think. Alec was trying to do you guys a favor, and maybe Mr. Duffy one, too."

Crider was talking to Chip now, looking directly at him, and there was scorn in his voice.

Chip's belligerence was completely gone, but he had nothing to say. He bent over the motor again.

Crider left, and I went over to get the gas cans.

When I came back, Chip was sitting in the car. He said, "After the Worthington, I'm going to see Dad, Elm."

I said nothing.

"I'm going to talk him into putting some money into our motor. Elm, we could swing it, with his money."

"Do what you think best, Chip," I said. "But it doesn't seem right, coming to him only when you need money, does it?"

"Probably not. And he'll want dear Cousin Harold in the deal, too, if he puts any money into it." He paused. "But that Duffy business was my fault. It's up to me to make up for that."

"One way to make up for it," I said, "is to show him who's the top man around here. A win in this one wouldn't do our cause any harm."

"I can't guarantee a win," Chip said, "but I guarantee you'll see some dust."

I saw some dust. I saw Chip take the lead after a vicious, crazy five-lap battle with Crider, and I saw that Crider wasn't going to take that without a struggle. Crider was a very, very clever boy at this game. He found a spot a few feet away from Chip's deck, and he rode that spot grimly, waiting for his chance.

He must have eaten a lot of dust. He must have thought it was raining pebbles. But he hung on, like the old man of the sea, waiting, waiting, waiting. . . .

Chip quickened the pace. Crider came along. The whole track, now, was obscured by the billowing dust. Vision was down to almost nothing. They didn't change the pace.

At thirty miles, it was Chip and Crider. At forty, fifty. . . . On the north curve, they swung wide, to lap a laggard, and for a breath-held moment, it didn't look as though they could make the groove again.

They were both going for the fence, sidewards, when the dust came down to blank out the picture.

I waited for the sounds of a crash, but none came. They came blasting out of the turn, Chip still leading.

Chip seemed to be gaining, in that stretch. Chip *was* gaining. He went into the south turn, all alone, thirty feet in front of Crider. He was running away, running wild. At sixty miles, he had more than a half lap lead. Crider had lost his tow.

I held the big sign up for Chip as he hurtled past, the prearranged signal that meant he should switch in the reserve tank.

I saw him gesture in reply. But then in the backstretch, the Marmon began to spit and falter, and flame shot out from the tail pipe.

Right then, I thought of the reserve tank. It couldn't be just coincidence that she'd start to miss

108

when the reserve gas poured in. And it couldn't be just coincidence that *only* the reserve gas was bad.

The Marmon went into the turn, still belching, still jerking, and was lost in the dust.

Crider went by, as Chip came out of the bend, hugging the rail. Crider was almost into the backstretch, as the Marmon limped into the pits. He was out of the race and there wasn't time to do anything about it.

Chip sat in the car, not moving, nor saying a thing, for moments. Finally, he said, "That was one of *my* bright ideas, wasn't it?" He shook his head. "I sure figure 'em out."

"Nothing wrong with the idea," I said. "But I'll bet you all the dough I own there was something wrong with the gas."

He looked up quickly. "What do you mean, Elm?"

"It didn't start to miss right away," I pointed out. "It didn't start to miss until that new gas got to the carburetor."

"That's right." He started to climb out, and stopped. "Elm, you think Crider might have—"

I shook my head. "If *anybody* tampered with those cans, it was somebody who knew which ones held the reserve gas. That's those two with the big spouts, over there. They hold exactly as much, together, as that tank. I always use them for that."

"But why just the reserve gas?" Chip asked. "Why not all of it?"

"We'd find out, right away, in that case. We'd have time to clean it out and get some more, before the race."

"Sure, sure," Chip said. He was out of the car, now. He was staring blankly at the gas cans. "But Elm, who—? If it isn't Crider, who would—"

"First," I said, "let's see if we're right. Let's see if there is water in that gas."

There was a pint or two left in the cans, and I poured it out onto the flat, rimmed edge of an inverted bucket. I could see the oily globules form, see them run like mercury over the flat surface. It was clear enough to me, and I looked at Chip. He nodded.

"But who—?" he said.

I thought about the spindle, the spindle that hadn't been greased. I said, "Maybe it was done before we left home."

"Jim Masker," Chip said.

I didn't answer.

"You mean him, don't you, Elm?"

"I was thinking of him," I admitted, "but it doesn't make sense. There'd be no reason for him to do a thing like this deliberately."

"How about Larry?"

Larry was the boy from school we'd hired. I

shook my head. "That doesn't make sense, either. They wouldn't do something like this without reason, would they? They're not crazy, either one of them."

"No," Chip said, "they're not crazy. They'd have to have some reason." He stopped talking, as two cars thundered by. Then, "Do you remember, Elm, when we came back from here, last time? Do you remember how surprised Jim was to find out *I'd* done the driving?"

I said I did. "But what does that prove?"

"I don't know," he said. "It just seemed strange, at the time. But I do know I'm going to have a talk with Jim Masker, when we get home."

I shook my head. "That won't do it. What can we prove? We're taking a long chance, even suspecting Jim. We'll need more than our suspicions for an accusation like that, Chip."

He agreed. We decided, finally, to say nothing to Jim when we got home. If what we suspected was true, an accusation now would only serve to warn him.

There's nothing artificial about Chip. You can tell how Chip feels, any time, by looking at his face. Jim must have read suspicion there, when we arrived home, next day.

The welcoming smile on his face looked spurious to me. He asked how the race had gone.

111

"Trouble, again," Chip said. "Carburetor trouble."

I thought I saw relief on Jim's face at the word "carburetor."

"I still think it was the gas," I said—and the face was instantly guarded.

I was sure, in my own mind, now. I didn't have anything a legal mind would call evidence, but I was as sure as I could be.

That night, we began to change the Marmon's gearing. The Worthington, as Chip had said, was no level run.

We worked late, and slept late the next day. We had scarcely finished breakfast when Mom told Chip there was somebody waiting for him down at the garage.

We went down together. When we passed the Mercedes in the yard, I knew who it was, and I started back for the house. But Chip said, "He hasn't got anything to say to me that you can't hear."

I went along.

Harold Adams was standing over near the Marmon, talking to Larry.

He smiled when he saw us. He said, "Oldfield and DePalma, I believe?"

"Not yet," Chip said. "The Mercedes giving you trouble, Harold?"

He looked puzzled a moment, then caught on. "Oh, no—I'm not here for service. Just thought I'd drop in and see if you've had a change of heart."

"I haven't," Chip said.

"Larry tells me your business has fallen off, this summer."

"Spring's always the best time," Chip explained. "When they pull their cars out of winter storage. Summer's bound to be slower."

Harold's casual manner was gone, now. He was dead serious when he said, "You're being very foolish, Chip. You're spoiling both our chances with this ridiculous enterprise."

Chip said nothing.

"It's grieved Elaine as deeply as it has your father," Harold went on. "You've deserted your friends. You're building castles in the air."

I didn't think any of this was my business. I went to the back of the shop, where Larry was scraping carbon out of a head.

"You shouldn't have told him about business falling off," I said quietly.

"I realize that, now," Larry said. "I wonder when you guys are going to realize *why* it's falling off."

"Why has it?"

Larry said, "It's not for me to criticize my superiors. But one thing the public expects, in a store or shop or *garage* is simple, everyday courtesy." He

113

had stopped scraping, now, and was looking directly at me.

"That's what we try to give them," I answered.

He shrugged. "Sure."

I put a hand on his arm. "You've got something more to say, Larry. Say it."

"I've said enough already," he answered. "I'm no stool pigeon."

"You mean, when we're not here, don't you, Larry?" I said. "That's what you meant?"

He took a deep breath, and went back to his scraping. "That's what I meant," he said.

Harold and Chip had gone outside, and were out of earshot, now. I said, "Don't tell Chip this, Larry. Chip's likely to let his temper get the best of him."

"All right," he said. "But I had to say something. You fellows have always treated me swell."

Outside, the voices were rising. Harold was getting angry. Harold was letting the thought of a quarter million dollars cut through his suavity. He said, "You're crazy, Chip. Do you think Elaine will be satisfied to be a garage mechanic's wife? Do you think she wouldn't appreciate the kind of money your father is prepared to put into—"

I started to run, when I heard that.

By the time I reached the yard, there was blood on Harold's mouth, and the big, blonde lad was closing in on Chip, his eyes nasty.

I stepped between them.

He stopped, then. I was too close to his own size. He said, "I'm sorry I lost my temper. But not nearly as sorry as you're going to be." He was climbing into the Mercedes, as I led Chip back to the garage.

Chip was trembling, and holding his skinned fist. I put an arm over his shoulders. "Slugger," I said, "when are you going to pick on somebody your own size? You're no heavyweight."

He grinned, and then he stopped grinning. He said, "We were looking for a reason, weren't we, Elm? We couldn't figure out—"

I knew what he meant. "I can't believe it," I said.

"Why not? If we don't make a go of it here, Harold would figure I'd come back to Dad. That's what he wants, more than anything in the world."

I thought of Jim closing up his small foundry, but refusing to sell it. Jim could collect wages from two employers—us, and Harold Adams. But I couldn't believe he'd deliberately clean a wheel bearing of its protective grease. That could be murder, and murder wouldn't serve Harold's purpose.

But he hadn't thought Chip was going to drive, that day. . . .

Chip asked, "Well, what do you think, Elm?"

"I think we ought to wait," I answered. "I think we should be real sure before we make an accusation like that."

115

"We don't need to make any accusation. We could just fire him."

"That wouldn't be fair," I said.

"He wanted us to quit racing. He was afraid we might make a go of it. He wanted us to bankrupt ourselves, buying a lot of new equipment. Good grief, Elm, what more do we need?"

"Something besides suspicion. We need some facts."

Jim came into the yard then, driving the tow truck. He'd been out on a tire repair job. I warned Chip, "Don't say anything. Saying something now would just put him on his guard."

"All right," Chip said. "But you can carry this fairness too far, Elm."

He was right about that. But I still don't think my way was wrong.

It was a bad time. Business was off, and so were our dispositions. We had our lowest income week of the summer, and two customers who had had ring jobs done came back to complain that their cars were using as much oil as ever.

I tore one of the motors down, and found out why. The cylinders were too badly worn to make a ring job successful; it needed new, oversized pistons.

That had been one of Jim's jobs.

I explained to the customer that it was new pistons he needed. He said I should have known that in the first place, and he'd be blazed if *this* shop was going to put in the new pistons. And what about the money he'd wasted on the former job?

I paid it all back.

I explained to Jim, as patiently as I could, how he had lost us a customer, a good customer.

He listened with the proper humility, and promised it wouldn't happen again. He certainly seemed sincere. Chip listened to all of it, saying nothing. When we were through, Chip shook his head, as if it were beyond his comprehension.

The other complaint was from the owner of a car on which Larry had worked. I took a chance on that, and explained to the customer that while the new rings are still stiff, before they're worn in, there's a chance the car will continue to use oil. If it wasn't corrected in the next couple of weeks, he could bring his car in and we would make amends. Free, of course.

It turned out that I was right. We didn't lose that customer.

The days went on; September was here. William Burgess swam the English Channel. Chip Adams and Elmer Ryan prepared to win the Worthington Cup.

The Marmon was right, all down the line. The gearing had been changed; there wasn't anything we could do to improve the motor. But we fiddled and fussed and tinkered and toiled, trying everything that made sense, and a few things that didn't. She would need to be a little better than her best, for the Worthington.

It wasn't actually a road race, this Worthington Cup, though a road made up part of it. And so did a treacherous four-mile run through the mountains, or what I like to think of as mountains, though some Westerners might give me an argument on that. In any event, there was a one-lane road through these —hills, and a sheer, unbroken drop of two thousand feet along a good part of the road.

It wasn't a road you'd want to travel at any speed, either up or down. The first time we made a final run, I was sorry I hadn't stayed home. As I explained to Chip, "We've really been neglecting that garage."

"We'll keep her in second, for this," Chip said. "I'm glad we geared up that second."

I wasn't.

After the mountain, the going was flat and straight for another four miles. Then the road doubled back and became a twisting snake. After that, it circled around the mountain, and went back where it came from. Why it didn't circle the mountain in the first place, I don't know. They tell me

118

one road was old, one new, and the two were combined for the contest.

It was less contest than test, a test of sanity. "It doesn't make sense," I told Chip. "It doesn't prove a thing."

But Chip wouldn't listen to sense. Chip had learned that Barney would be here, for this one. It was like talking to a wall, after that.

"You don't have to ride along, you know, Elm," he said. "You'd be crazy, if you came along, just for the ride."

"No crazier than you are," I answered.

"Well," he said, "I can't tell you why exactly, Elm, but I won't back down now."

"In that case," I said, "I'll go along—just for the ride." Then I added, "And I hope Barney runs you into the ground."

"Want to bet?" he asked me, grinning.

"I never bet a cinch," I told him.

We rode it a few times after that, studying it. The best strategy, we decided, would be to get to these mountains *first*. There was a three-mile straightaway, before the climb started; there would be no passing anywhere on the grade. But the car that got here first would have the advantage of setting the pace for four miles.

It was an excellent idea. The only thing really wrong with it was that it didn't work.

For there were five cars in the line-up ahead of us, fast cars, all of them, and driven by five men who had the same idea we had, to get to the mountains first.

We stayed with them, while they fought it out. We didn't lose an inch, nor gain one. Their collective and individual battles effectively blocked the road, and there wasn't a thing Chip could do about that except grumble. He wasn't smiling, this day.

All the way to the grade, we trailed them, and they went into single file. There may have been some changes ahead, but there was none for us. We still rode sixth.

Now for the monotonous climb, I thought. Now for the low speed stuff. I thought.

The man in the car ahead of us was crazy. I watched him hit the first twisting bend, about a hundred feet up. At any sane speed, it was a perfectly safe turn. But this maniac hit it so fast, he started to slide, sending a shower of grit over the abrupt edge.

That's Nelson's car, I thought. *He's victory-hungry. He's lost his mind.*

Chip gunned into the curve. I heard gravel rolling; I saw the grit fan out, and felt the lurch. I took one frightened glimpse over the edge of my seat, and saw the tops of the tall pines, far below, reaching for me. . . .

"Chip, for God's sake—"

And we were clear, for the moment, inches from the cliff wall to our left. I breathed again. I felt the nausea stirring in me.

Ahead, there was another curve. Ahead, there was no car in sight. *They're all crazy,* I thought, *every last one of them, victory-crazy.*

We slid into the second curve, toward the brink. Then, just as we seemed destined to hurtle off into space, Chip swung the wheel over hard. Again, we skidded toward the haven of the cliff wall.

There was too much mechanic in me for this. Steering gears break, at times, I knew. Steering knuckles crack, and brakes fail, and tires blow. And drivers make quarter-inch mistakes in safety allowance. Any driver, even the best, even Chip.

Again, there was no car in sight as we cleared the turn. The men ahead knew this route, had raced it before. They knew where to save time.

The Marmon was still driving, still gunning. Chip's face was as tight as a drumhead. His eyes, under the goggles, were unreadable.

I looked at his hands on the wheel, at his heavy wrists, unbelievably powerful for so slim a lad. My stomach was empty-feeling, and growling. I tried to concentrate on Chip's wrists, I tried to think back on all the close ones they'd pulled me through, and pulled himself through.

We'd had two accidents in our first two races. We hadn't had a flat tire, under competition, since that first race, last year. I tried to figure all the odds.

But my mind kept coming back to here and now, to the timbered slopes, far, far below, to Chip, determined to get *some* car in sight. To Chip, who had forgotten any caution he may have had.

Another curve, another lurch towards eternity. I kept my eyes open this time. I forced myself to stare at the trees below. There weren't any individual trees to make out, now, there was just a green carpet. We were *up*.

We were, as a matter of fact, at the top.

There was only one way to go, now—down. But there were two ways to travel it. One on the road, and one over the edge.

Going up, we'd been under power, we'd had the grade itself as a brake. Going down, we'd have only our compression and the brakes. And what caution Chip chose to use.

There was a knot of spectators up here. I wanted to join them. This would be a fine race—to watch.

We were rolling, down-grade, as Chip shifted into *high*. I said nothing. He was the driver; his was the decision. But that helped to eliminate one of the safety factors, the compression. And it told me the other hadn't been a factor at all—Chip's caution. From here in, it would be my brakes and his skill.

I was glad I'd relined the brakes.

We finally caught a glimpse of Red Nelson's job, as we slued around the first curve. Red was going slower, now. Red was getting smarter. Chip barreled down toward him.

The worst curve in the mountain route was coming up. If we got past this one, I thought, the rest couldn't be too bad. Nelson was again out of sight, as we rolled down toward the curve below. Nelson was in the curve, or just around it, or. . . . I tried not to think of that.

Chip was going too fast. His memory is bad, I thought. This is a near-hairpin coming up, a narrow, twisting devil of a curve, and Nelson just might be in it, traveling slowly.

We went into it straight, and directly toward the outer rim, as usual. Again, I saw the pines reaching. Again, I saw Chip swing the wheel over hard.

But this time, the Marmon didn't respond as quickly. She began to tilt, as Chip went for the brakes, as he used both brakes and power in a frantic effort for a controlled spin.

For what seemed like seconds, but couldn't have been, the Marmon teetered there, on the razor-edge of disaster.

I opened my mouth; I'll never know why, and I saw the ridge of muscle in Chip's ungauntleted wrists knot up, as he fought the Marmon's perversity. It was man against machine, in that second, for the highest stakes in the world.

The spin came, finally. My prayers went up with the dust that billowed out over the edge of the abyss.

Directly below was Nelson. And directly below Nelson was God's level ground. Not one more curve to travel before we hit the level ground. It was like a song in my mind, a joyous song.

All right, Chip Adams, I thought, *scare me now. Do your best, you black-haired devil, you undersized genius. We're through the mountains; scare me now.*

I will say this for him; he came close to doing it. He certainly tried, on the long stretches that were left, on the reverse and double and triple reverse curves that were still to be traveled.

We caught Red, in that four-mile straightaway. We caught Merz, there, too. Straight stuff, pure speed, and the Marmon had it. Even I could have done as well, there.

We caught Hitchcock, the mountain specialist, just past the first curve on the winding return to the mountain.

That made three of them. That meant there were only two ahead. The first of the two we overtook was Hunter, and Hunter had lived most of his life just a mile from this part of the road.

That's when Chip almost scared me again. I would have been scared, but anything after that mountain run just had to be an anticlimax.

Hunter had a high-wheel rebuilt Apperson and it was a straightaway speedster, the fastest straight run job in the contest. Hunter had more courage than sense. On the curves, he had no sense at all.

But that's where Chip caught him, finally, on a curve. The Apperson went into it low, and slued wide. Chip, riding the Apperson's deck, went into it higher, and fought for the groove.

The Marmon was sluing, too, but it was a controlled slide, with forward traction. The Marmon came out of the turn first, and there were plenty of turns ahead.

Chip gained, there. He gained plenty. Hunter, I'm sure, went into those curves faster than we did, but Hunter, I know, didn't complete them nearly as well as Chip. For we gained, on every curve. We would need that advantage. On the straightaway finish, I knew, the high-wheeled Apperson would have the advantage.

Curves to the right, to the left, and the Marmon teetering on every one, while I wondered about the tires. They were taking a terriffic beating.

Around the mountain now. I looked up at it, and contemplated thumbing my nose. But it wouldn't be dignified, I decided. It wouldn't be proper for the riding mechanic of America's most daring and insane pilot.

Around the mountain, and the long, straight stretch to home. Ahead, dust funneled up from the one car between us and the checkered flag.

This seemed familiar. This was a situation I *knew* I'd been in before. This, I then remembered, was a replica of the Grand National. It had been DePalma, that time, but otherwise, the situation was identical.

With my violetlike modesty, I realized that once again it would be a test of motors, of mechanical fitness.

I didn't need a glance at Chip's face to know who that was ahead. But I glanced at him, just the same, and he wasn't smiling, for a change.

It would be thrilling to recount a hub and hub battle, a one-inch victory to the checkered flag. To recount a tale of straining motors and anxious drivers and a two-car hippodrome finish.

But the Marmon would have none of that. The Marmon, in an apologetic effort for its perversity on that last mountain turn, didn't run. It flew.

We caught Barney a good quarter mile from the flag, and went past him on invisible wings. We sailed across the line all alone, and going away. That Marmon. . . .

It put Chip up there, for the year, all right. They

knew about Chip Adams, now. They even knew about Elmer Ryan, some of them. It took us a day to arrange for shipping the Marmon home. We followed it two hours later.

We didn't have much to say to each other, on the trip. We'd had a good season, a fine, successful season. It didn't seem the proper time to remember that our objective had not been attained, that no sporting gentleman with a fortune was begging to support our project.

Well, a man can do no more than his best. We can't all be Louis Chevrolet, I reasoned.

Chip was still in a partial glow from beating Barney. Chip wasn't looking as unhappy as he would, in the days to come.

He said, "We've got some races ahead of us yet. I'm not quitting, this year, Elm."

"That was the end of the season, for us," I said. "You promised Elaine—"

"That's the end of *one* season," he answered. "I promised Elaine I'd quit when we'd accomplished what we set out to do."

"Sometimes it's hard, explaining things to women."

"I know," he said. "And especially Elaine."

And especially Elaine. . . . Chip went to see her, the day after we arrived home.

When Chip came back, he looked lost. He said,

"Elm, something's happened, something I can't believe." He held out his hand.

I looked at the diamond sparkling there, the ring he'd given her just a few months before.

"It'll blow over," I said. "All people in love quarrel. She'll change her mind."

"I hope so. But—even if she doesn't, Elm, I can't go back to—to what she expects. We've got to go ahead with our plans." He seemed to be seeking my confirmation. "Isn't that the only way? Don't you feel it is?"

"I do," I said, "but we can both be wrong, you know, Chip. I've nothing to lose. You're the boy who's fighting the odds. You're turning your back on a guaranteed future."

"Don't remind me of that," he said. "I'm thinking about it too much already."

That was in September. We went back to school, that month, but we arranged our classes so one of us could be in the garage mornings, the other afternoons.

Some of our business came back. We were quite well known locally, now, and there were quite a few satisfied customers that Jim had never had occasion to meet. We wouldn't get rich, but we made a living.

Jean came back to town the last part of September. Her Reo was in the yard one afternoon when I came back from a service call. She looked great. She would never have Elaine's beauty, but she looked awfully good to me that fall afternoon.

"It's been a long time," I said, "and sad, too."

"I'll bet you didn't even notice I was gone," she said, "either one of you." She was smiling.

"I did," I said, "and Chip often speaks of you."

Her smile dimmed. "Is it true, Elm, what I hear about Chip and Elaine? Did—she break the engagement?"

I nodded. "It's only temporary though, I hope. Don't you think it's only temporary?"

"I don't know," she said. "Sometimes, I can't figure Elaine out. Sometimes, I think I don't know her at all."

I went in with her, then, to see Mom. I told her about the summer's races, about beating DePalma and Barney, and she seemed to get as much enjoyment out of it as we had.

Chip came home from school. Chip asked, casually, "Jean, have you seen Elaine at all lately?"

The pain in his eyes didn't match the casualness of his voice. Jean said she hadn't seen Elaine for very long, just a few minutes since her return.

There was a silence.

Jean broke it, finally. She said, "Elaine's headstrong, at times. But she gets over it. She'll get over this, Chip." She tried a smile, and couldn't quite

129

make it. She looked at me for support, but there wasn't anything I could add to that.

She left, soon after.

"A lovely girl," Mom said, "a really fine young woman."

"Elm's lucky," Chip agreed.

"Me?" I said. "Don't get any ideas about me, not that way. She's just a friend." I don't think either one of them believed me.

According to the newspapers, Judge Adams had resumed his public speeches. But in less than two months, Teddy was to break his silence, incited by Taft's dissolution suit against the United States Steel Corporation. For two years and eight months, Teddy had made no disparaging comment regarding President Taft. But after his reply to Taft, in the *Outlook*, November 16, any hope Judge Adams might have had for party unity was certainly dispelled. The Colonel was not one to mince words.

It was a sad sight. Two honest and public-spirited men, one-time friends, engaging in a vicious, name-calling battle of thoughtless words and political strategy. It was a bad time for the party and for the nation.

Judge Adams was just a straw in the whirlwind, a man of principle without flexibility, a man of integrity without tolerance, of reason without vision.

He covered the state on a speaking tour, pleading

for a return to what he called "basic party principles." What he probably meant were *his* principles.
He was a small man in a big fight.

It was a nasty winter, and the Judge was an
elderly man. He lacked the stamina for a speaking
program as demanding as the one he attempted.

For the second time, he contracted pneumonia.

Two days before Christmas, he died. He died a
bitter, unforgiving man. Before his illness he had
composed a new will, cutting Chip completely out
of any inheritance in the estate. Every bit of property, real and personal, *everything* went to his
nephew, Harold Adams.

Dear Cousin Harold. . . .

It wasn't the money. Chip had, by his own choice,
forfeited his right to that. It was the thought that
his own father should carry the thought of venge-
ance to such lengths.

Chip was a sick boy, for a while, after that. He'd
been hit twice, hit hard, in the last few months. He
was a boy with a lot of heart, and that's where he'd
been hit. We never talked of it. I had no words to
match the depth of his grief and Chip volunteered
none.

The day after the reading of the will, Jim Masker
quit. Any doubts I may have had about his treach-
ery were dispelled by that action. He could serve no
further purpose for Cousin Harold in our employ.

Larry said, "Well, at least we know, now. At least he won't be able to hurt you any more."

I thought Larry was right about that. I had no reason to think otherwise, at the time.

Chip was a working fool that winter. I couldn't keep up with him. He didn't expect me to keep up with him. Work was the only release he had for the turbulence that must have been bubbling inside him. We had a lot of cars to prepare for storage, although we didn't have the space to store them ourselves. Most of the local citizens still hadn't the audacity to run their cars through one of our winters.

We hired a friend of Larry's from school to take Jim's place. Our business was coming back. We hoped it would bring in enough to maintain our racing schedule for the year. This would be the year, we told ourselves. Even J. Ellington Duffy wouldn't be able to ignore us this year.

Wilbur Wright died that year, and Clara Barton, and Lord Lister. Teddy was shot at in Milwaukee, but he finished the speech he was making, his shirt front sodden with blood. And on her maiden journey, the *Titanic* struck an iceberg. Only 705 people were saved of the more than two thousand on board.

In the New York *Sun,* early in January, appeared an advertisement for the revolutionary new Disco

Self-Starter. It was, the ad read, safe, sure and simple. It would make your car self-starting and up-to-date in the three hours necessary to install it.

Larry, who had shown me the ad, said, "It looks like the automobile is here to stay. This is bigger than the coaster brake on the bike."

It was still a speculative business, however. It wasn't anything you'd think would interest a young man as sensible and cautious as Harold Adams. But that was the rumor which persisted in town.

And an addition was being built on Jim Masker's foundry.

We didn't connect these two things, nor did we connect either of them with us. The less we heard about those two gentlemen, the better we liked it.

We planned for the summer. All through the dragging, miserable winter, we lived for the day when we could get the Marmon out onto the road again.

It was in March, the last part of March, that Chip and I saw the connection between the rumor about Harold Adams and the addition to Jim Masker's foundry.

Cousin Harold was financing Jim in the production of an automobile engine, to be named the Adams Engine. With the advent of summer, the Masker plant would be still further enlarged, and the Adams car would be launched, after that. In the meantime, reported the local paper, the foundry was busy, filling the unprecedented flood of orders for the new motor.

It didn't seem logical to me that Jim Masker had the stuff to design an automobile engine. Harold must have hired some engineers.

Late in April, the school received one of the motors, as a gift from the Adams Corporation. It was a cut-away model, to be used in primary study of internal combustion engines. Chip and I were beyond that, but we examined it, just the same.

We didn't have to examine it long to see that it was *our* motor.

Chip said, "Shall we hire a lawyer, or buy a gun?"

"Let's see a lawyer first," I suggested.

The lawyer we saw was old Jed Abel, who occupied a dusty, dim office over the Bon Ton Haberdashery. Jed had been executor of the Adams estate. He was a thin and short-tempered old man, as frugal as he was honest.

We explained it all in detail, and he didn't miss a word, his bright old eyes moving from my face to Chip's and back. When we'd finished, he said, "They copied some specifications, that's the gist of it, isn't it?"

That was about it, we agreed.

His smile was tight. "I can write them a letter, and maybe throw a scare into them. And maybe not." He coughed dryly. "What I'm trying to say, gentlemen, is that you haven't got a case."

"You mean," Chip asked, "that we, as inventors, can't protect our own invention?"

"You aren't inventors," Mr. Abel said. "The gasoline motor was invented a long time ago. You did *design* a particular engine with certain specifications. I'm not familiar enough with the patent laws, offhand, to know whether specification can be patented. In any event, you *didn't* attempt to patent this motor. I presume the current manufacturers may also have neglected to do so?"

We didn't know, and we told him that.

"Well, there's a reasonable chance that you can go right ahead and produce *your* motor. There's nothing to prevent you from doing that, is there?"

"Nothing important," Chip said bitterly. "Only money."

Mr. Abel shrugged. "Chip, I'll be frank enough to admit I wasn't too happy about my position as executor in your father's estate. But I consoled myself with the knowledge that you were doing very well in your own right. You've established quite a reputation, young man, and not only locally. I'm sure, if there's no legal barrier to your producing this motor, money won't prove to be an obstacle for long."

"Perhaps not," Chip said. "But the more I do to

135

build up the Adams name, the more free advertising Harold will get. It's logical for people to think a car made in this town, named the Adams Four, has something to do with me and Elm."

"I hadn't thought of that," Mr. Abel said.

And neither had I. But it made sense, too much sense.

We left the office, sadder and no wiser. "It's a good motor," I said to Chip. "There was really only one thing wrong with it—it needed an eighth of an inch more bore."

"Aw, Elm—" he said.

"All right," I said, "we'll take it lying down, if that's what you want. But you know we can improve on it. You know we're a long way from licked. We've got the garage, and your reputation. We've got the Marmon."

"I ought to go over and—"

"No," I said. "We'll beat him at his own game, Chip. That's the only kind of beating he can understand. He'll sink his money in this plant, and once we're in production, we'll—"

"Once we're in production—" he said. "When do you figure *that* will be, Elm?"

"It could be next month," I answered, "or it could be never. I know we won't get anywhere by quitting."

"I wasn't planning on quitting," he said. "Let's

136

go over to the *Courier* office. I've got an ad I'd like to run."

I thought he had an ad for the garage in mind, but I was wrong. It was less advertisement than announcement. It stated that the motor designed by the racing team of Elmer Ryan and Chip Adams was not yet in production. Chip Adams, it stated further, was in no way connected with a corporation presently manufacturing motors under that name or a similar name. The motor designed by Chip Adams and Elmer Ryan would be available as soon as circumstances permitted.

It was a gentlemanly, dignified announcement and was open to any interpretation the reader might be inclined to make. It didn't actually state that Cousin Harold was trading on the Adams' name, but those in the business could conceivably read that into it.

After its one appearance in the local *Courier*, we ordered some of the announcements for mailing.

Fighting with words, and words were about all we had right now. I suppose you'd call it psychological warfare. Neither of us thought much of it as a weapon, but we *had* to strike back, however weakly.

We had another block cast—with a larger bore. We stepped up the compression a bit, and improved the manifolding. We got the lightest weight cast iron pistons available. Aluminum pistons were something for the future, but we got as close to their weight as any car manufactured.

It was a better motor, we agreed. Even if it hadn't been, we'd have thought it was. But this *was.*

We mailed quite a lot of the announcements to all the friends we'd made in the racing game, to parts manufacturers and body builders, to the entire trade. A lot of the motor cars being produced at that time were what is known as "assembled" cars. The body would be built by one manufacturer, the motor by another. The final producer of the car may have done little more than fit together the assembled parts and give it a name.

I didn't think much of the system. We would sell our motor only if we had to. I preferred building the entire car.

We got a lot of inquiries. Most of them asked for tentative prices on the new motors, and tentative delivery dates. We answered these as honestly as possible, mentioning the difficulty of getting manufacturing facilities. We didn't explain that our biggest difficulty was a lack of money. There is an American myth, it seems, that famous people are rich people. We didn't dispel the myth.

How all this affected Harold Adams, we didn't discover until later. There were rumors about Harold's business falling off. A few of the replies we received indicated that at least some in the trade had thought the Adams Engine was a Chip Adams product.

Garage customers who had been offended by Jim Masker's rudeness began to come again for service. Our announcement in the local paper had put us on the other side of the fence from Jim.

It was a soggy, chilly, and unseasonable spring. We would have a warm day, a day that would prophesy more of the same, and we'd start planning on a road tryout for the Marmon. Then it would snow.

It was snowing the night I saw the light in the garage.

It had been a restless night. After tossing and turning for a few hours, I got up and went to the window. Outside, wet flakes were falling, though the temperature was above freezing. The roads would be sloppier than ever.

I saw the flash of light in the back of the garage, and then it disappeared. Chip—? No, Chip had gone to bed when I did. If he were down there, the lights would be on. The same applied to Larry.

I put on some clothes, and went quietly down the steps and out to the yard. Again, from here, I thought I saw a flash of light.

Then I thought I'd been foolish to come down here alone. If this was a prowler, the reasonable thing to do was to get help, or call the police. I didn't feel reasonable. I'd had enough trouble lately to make me want a little personal, physical revenge.

I was very quiet, unlocking the garage door. The key made no noise. I swung the door wide, and the hinges groaned. I was staring into darkness, silence and darkness. There was an overpowering odor of gasoline in the air.

I took one step into the darkness and then I heard the noise, something like the scrape of a shoe on the rough flooring. I stopped, and called, "Who's there?"

There was no answer, but I heard the scrape again, and experienced that intuitive feeling of someone near. I sensed, rather than saw, the dark blob to my right, and I turned quickly that way.

There was a rush of air past my face, and pain flashed up from my shoulder. That quick turn of my head had possibly saved my life. The blow intended for my skull was vicious and heavy. I half turned and went down, under the force of it, and the shape moved past me, toward the door.

I heard a clatter of something dropping, and instinctively I reached to pick it up. It was a heavy, adjustable wrench.

I still had it in my hand when I regained my feet, and started out the open doorway, after the prowler. He didn't head for the road, but cut directly across the drive, toward the open field to the east of the garage.

I was still shaky, and the going was slow. Less than halfway across that muddy field, I realized my assailant was gaining. I turned back.

I turned just in time to see the great "whoosh" of flame shatter the windows of the garage.

The rest is a confusion of vivid memories. I remember the glow of fire against the sky, and the greasy smell of the black smoke. I remember the fire wagons clanging into the yard, the horses nervous and restless against the bright glare. I remember how the firemen worked to prevent the fire from spreading to the house, and how they finally succeeded. I remember having to hold Chip from dashing into that hell to save the Marmon.

And I remember when there was nothing but the smoking stench of embers left, that Mom made coffee for the firemen, and that she tried to console Chip and me. We were insured, she reminded us. Oh, sure, we were insured. . . .

A man named Mike Stevens, a stranger from

New York, sat in our parlor asking questions. He was an investigator for the Avon Insurance Company. He was a neat, quiet and well-built man of about forty, with a high, stiff collar and a very practical air about him.

There would be, he told us, some delay in settling the claims we had on his company. In fires of "possibly incendiary origin" it was company policy to complete an investigation before claims were satisfied.

"Possibly incendiary?" Chip repeated bitterly. "I'll give you even money I could name the man behind it, right now. I could give you a motive, too. You don't think *we* set fire to that garage, do you? You don't think we had anything to gain by it?"

"In my business," Mike Stevens said, "I don't guess. I dig for what facts there are, and submit them to the company. From what I've dug out of this affair so far, it looks like arson, all right. There was a timing device, set for thirty seconds, and from the fire department's reports it appears that the interior of the garage had been soaked with gasoline. But you say this prowler you saw had a light on in the building?"

"Only in the back part of the shop," I said, "in the room where we store the oil. If it was matches he was using, he was safe enough in there."

"You're getting ahead of me," Mike Stevens said quietly.

I matched his tone of voice. "No, I'm not. I can see what you were suggesting. Do you think I hit myself in the shoulder, too?"

He shook his head. "I'm not thinking either way. Right now, I'm after facts. I have the wrench, and I've sent it to be checked for possible fingerprints. The tracks in the snow are all drifted over, but there's a fine, clear footprint in the clay of the field." He paused. "A print that isn't yours, I've discovered. When I get all of the information I can, the company will decide what to do." He rose.

"When you get all the information you can," Chip said, "you can tie it to Jim Masker, the vice-president of the Adams Engine Company. You could save yourself a lot of work if you picked him up, right now."

We had told Stevens all about our suspicions of Jim, everything, from the dry spindle incident to his stealing our motor specifications. He had listened attentively, but I couldn't tell how much of our story he believed.

Now, he turned to me. "Are you willing to testify in court, under oath, that the man you chased through the fields was Mr. Masker?"

I shook my head. "I'm willing to testify that he looked a lot like Mr. Masker, though."

"That isn't enough," Mike Stevens said. He frowned. "Gentlemen, I can understand your feelings in this matter. But let me give you one word of warning. Say nothing of your suspicions to *anyone*. If Mr. Masker is guilty, we don't want him forewarned." Again, he paused. "And if he isn't guilty, you don't want a libel suit on your hands."

Chip started to say something, but I interrupted. "We'll play along, Mr. Stevens. We'll say no more about it." I put a hand on Chip's shoulder. I could feel him tremble.

It had been a bad winter for Chip Adams.

We didn't have a garage, and the Marmon was ruined. We had nothing but our reputations, and those wouldn't win us any races. At the supper table that night, Chip said, "What next? Maybe we can find jobs, somewhere, and—"

"Jobs?" Mom said. "You're going to race this year, aren't you? You're not quitting now, I hope?"

I told her that the insurance money was being held up, and that the Marmon was ruined beyond repair.

She sniffed. "You don't think I've been wasting your money, do you, Elmer Ryan? Did you think I haven't been putting it away for you?"

She wasn't talking about any money of mine, I

144

knew. She was thinking about her nest egg, the insurance Dad had left added to what she'd managed to save, through the years.

"I don't want it, Mom," I said.

"There'll be no talk about that," she told me. "It's yours, to do with as you see fit. You'll work in no factory, Elmer Ryan, not while I'm alive."

I took it, finally. Or rather, we both took it, Chip and I. We decided not to buy another car to re-vamp. We planned to build our own this time, from the ground up.

We called it the Ryan-Adams Speedway Four. If you think that's a fancy name, remember some of the others of that time and later—the Stutz Bearcat, the Paige Daytona, the Apperson Jack Rabbit, the Jordan Playboy, the Wills St. Claire Gray Goose Traveler.

Those were magic names, names for men's dreams. The cars are dead now, but nothing will ever kill the dreams. Colonel Howard Marmon, too, was to go out of the automobile business in the thirties, after his sixteen-cylinder engineering masterpiece won him an S.A.E. award. It's a strange game. I've been in it for a long time, but I'll never understand it. Some of its top minds, its best men have died penniless, while some of its manipulators, its medicine men have made millions. A fascinating, heartbreaking, unpredictable game.

Ours wasn't too fantastic a name, especially with the "Ryan" in it. And, if we were successful, it would be a good name for our proposed car.

We cast another block, with just a shade more stroke. We kept the same manifolding and the same bore. For the racing car, we used a higher compression head. Otherwise, it was our regular motor.

Spring, in its perverse way, decided to arrive early that year. The roads were dry, the sun warm. We tried not to notice. The Marmon was a charred and ugly wreck, and the road was no longer beckoning to her.

We worked. We got hardly any sleep, but we never seemed to feel tired, because this was work we loved.

The last part of May we had her ready for the road, the Ryan-Adams Speedway Four. It was a low-hung, rounded, glistening beauty.

Since that time I've made a dollar or two, and won a few awards. But I have never achieved anything, or shared in any endeavor that gave me as much personal pride and satisfaction as I felt that May day.

We stood staring at it mutely. Then Chip went into the house.

When he came out, he was carrying our goggles.

The sun was warm and the road hard. The little

red car moved along it like a cat, sure-footed, purring. Then Chip gave her the spurs.

I heard the rasp of gravel as the wheels dug, and felt her fight for traction. I felt her soar, as she found it. We were flying. She was all we'd hoped for. She was a road-hugging, throttle-sensitive, power-packed sweetheart. With Chip Adams at the wheel, we were going to be very, very hard to beat, this year.

It was while we were coming back from that first trial run that we saw the black car, going the other way. It was long and low, a race job, and it was really making time. Dust enveloped us, as it blasted by.

The dust, however, didn't obscure one of the two occupants of the car. Chip said, "Jim Masker. What the—"

"Jim Masker," I agreed. "I wonder what it's all about?"

We found out, the next day. The Adams Engine Corporation had hired Red Nelson to pilot the Adams Special in all the year's major races, as a part of the new promotional policy of the Corporation.

I want to say this about Red, he had all the nerve any man needs. He'd had some lean years and some bad luck, but you'll find him in the records just the same. I learned later that the Corporation

147

had approached Barney and DePalma first, but they had interpreted our announcement correctly, and they turned the Corporation down. How many other topnotchers had turned them down, I don't know.

Red didn't. Red had played it alone for years, with inadequate equipment and financing. Maybe he was a little fed up with playing it alone.

I hated to see Red on that side of the fence, but there wasn't anything we could do about that. Harold probably figured he could further confuse the public by putting a car on the track labeled with a famous name. And that black, low devil was a lot of car.

But we'd be in the same races, with a better car, and a better driver. And, of course, a better mechanic in the pits.

The first time we tangled with Red and the Adams Special was at Meadow Bay, in June. It was a hundred-mile run for the Eastern Division title, and it was something we wanted badly. Not only for the prestige involved; we were on thin ice, financially, and we needed to win.

The Meadow Bay oval was a well-banked dish, a mile long, and designed for automobiles. This was no converted horse-race track. The pits were protected, the officials intelligent, and the strip well maintained. But it was still a dirt track, and just as treacherous in a long run as any county fair layout.

A hundred miles on dirt is a long run, today, or then. The dirt piles up in places, and the track becomes rough and tricky as the wheels go to work on it. Today there are plenty of good boys who avoid the grit ovals, and I don't blame them. In those days, most of them were dirt, and we couldn't be so choosy.

It was like coming home, seeing the gang again at Meadow Bay. Dawson, who'd just won the five hundred, Jenkins, Mulford, Wilcox . . . ragging us about our new car with the fancy name, joshing us about putting the Marmon out to pasture.

Red said "Hello" and nothing more. He had probably been briefed. There was no sign of Cousin Harold or Jim Masker.

The second day we were there, Chip qualified the Speedway Four, and set a new one-lap record doing it. That won him the inside spot, on the pole. Red flanked him. Red had missed tying the record by a tenth of a second, with less car. He had gone crazy, for a lap.

Wilcox said to me, "Red's changed, you know it? He seems like a man possessed."

"He's had some bad seasons," I answered. "You really can't blame him, if he's a little sour."

149

"That's no attitude to take onto a track," Howie said. "He's not alone out there."

Red knew he wasn't alone, all right. Red knew whom he had to beat.

It was a warm day, with a faint breeze. The stands were full, the infield dotted here and there with groups of standing spectators. Then, the familiar thunder from the speed wagons as they moved around for the flying start, their colors glinting in the sun.

The red car and the black car in the first row, leading the parade. The Adams' cars—Chip's and mine, and Cousin Harold's. Jockeying, in the first row, for position, jockeying all along the line, and the first faint stirrings of dust rising in the warm air.

The smell of oil burning, and the increasing roar. The flag held high. Everybody standing, everybody tense. Including Elmer Ryan, in the pits.

The flag dropping, the sigh from the spectators, the red car and the black car battling into the turn. Both of them wide open, both their drivers determined the test would be *here*.

The fans remained on their feet.

Chip had the fence and the groove, and a hairbreadth more speed under the hood. They both went into it sliding high. Chip still had the inside, and he was under control. He led Nelson out of the turn by five feet.

That lead varied, in the next few laps, but he never gained more than thirty feet. Red was out to get him.

It was a good race to watch, if you were just a spectator. If you didn't know they were traveling way beyond the traction limit, both of them. If you're the kind who likes to see disaster shaping up, it was a fine race.

I stood in the pits and cursed both of them. Chip wouldn't cut down, I knew, while Red pressed him. What common sense Red might have possessed in the past had deserted him now. He was out to win, and he couldn't win while Chip led him.

The track was torn to shreds in the first thirty miles. There were other speedsters in that race besides the two leaders, and they were determined not to be outclassed.

Lap after lap, it went on, a mad merry-go-round of racket and dust and careening cars. In the pits, we were silently watching, silently waiting.

With ten laps to go, with the track a sea of ridged dirt, Chip still rode first, and he was leading Red by a good thirty feet. Maybe he realized how dangerous his speed was. I couldn't notice any slackening of his pace, but Red was gaining.

In five laps, Red climbed up to a challenging position. With only five to go, they were rubbing hubs into the south turn. Chip still had the inside, and the advantage. He fought off the challenge all around the bend, and began to pull away in the backstretch.

He had increased his lead to ten feet as they plowed into the north curve.

Red would have caught him there, if he hadn't been on the high side. They both came out sidewards, blanketing that end of the stands with grit and dust.

In the front stretch, Chip gained again. In the bend, Red almost caught him. Red was riding those turns at a pace way beyond reason. He knew it was his only chance to catch the red car. We had too much for him on the straightaway.

Three laps to go, two, one. . . .

In the backstretch, they lapped a laggard. Into the north turn, Red was again almost climbing Chip's deck. They both rode high, this time, fighting the skid, powering for the groove.

Chip found it first, and he was three feet from the fence when Red started to come down. The nose of the black job was pointed directly down-track, now. Red didn't have the clearance to go by, and it's a cinch Chip wasn't going to slow down to give him clearance. The black job kept coming.

There was another car, the car they'd lapped, directly behind them now. If Red didn't pull clear soon. . . .

Red had no intention of pulling clear. He was going to make it a test of courage. I knew even the slightest bump would slow both of them enough so that the car behind would crash. I remembered Howie saying, "He's not alone out there."

I hoped Chip would remember that. I hoped Chip had some conscience left, even if Red hadn't.

I saw the black car pounding down, closer, closer—and I saw Chip slow down, to give him clearance. Red rode the one spot.

In the last few hundred yards, Chip tried to go around, as Red settled in the groove. He pulled up even with Red's rear wheels—as they thundered past the checkered flag.

It was Red's race, and Red's title.

When they idled into the pits, a lap later, Chip was as taut as a bowstring. His face was black with dirt and oil and his eyes blazed from the white area the goggles had covered.

"You see that?" he asked me.

I nodded. "You were thinking of the car behind, weren't you?"

"That's right. But what will the others think? They'll think I'm yellow. They'll think I showed

the feather. I'm going over to talk to that butcher."
He started to get out.

"No, you're not," I said. "You're going to stay right here. I'm going over to talk to him." I shoved him down again in his seat.

Red was still sitting in his car, talking to his pit monkeys. I said, "One more like that, and you'll answer to me. If that ever happens again, I'll take you apart."

He didn't look too frightened. He said, "What happens again? Winning, you mean?"

"You know what I mean," I told him. "I'm warning you, Red."

He said, "Chip afraid to talk up for himself?"

"No. Chip was going to come back. He'd probably have brought a wrench along. Chip isn't as easy-going as I am. He'd have killed you, probably, Red." I left him with that.

Chip asked, "What'd he say?"

I didn't tell him. I said, "He won't do it again, I'll bet."

"He'd better not," Chip said. "Next time I won't worry about the car behind."

It became a bitter duel, after that, between Chip and Red. That's no good on the speedway. There's enough danger, enough disaster without making each race a personal battle. But Chip wasn't listening to that kind of advice.

Springfield was next. Springfield was murder.

Chip made a farce out of it. He would let Red climb up to within challenging distance, and then the little red car would sprout wings.

It was a thing to see. On a track heavy with piled dust, in a race more than half filled with local jalopies, Chip wove in and out, lapping the local boys, playing tag with Red Nelson.

He was flirting with death. Some of the local boys were in their first season, some in their first race. Their equipment wasn't what it should be. A flat tire, on one of those curves. . . .

It was a thing to see, all right, but not with pleasure.

With five laps to go, and Chip enjoying a half lap lead, Red went after him in earnest. The black car soared up into the nightmare level, seeming to eat the distance to Chip. With three laps to go, Red was less than a hundred feet behind.

Again, Chip let him climb. Again, Chip waited for the challenge. And again he met it with a spurt of speed. He pulled away from Red, but not much. Not nearly enough for comfort.

Red had the black demon revved right up to her flaming limit. Chip kept gaining, but you'd have needed a ruler to measure it. Chip kept inching away, almost imperceptibly adding to the daylight between them.

Red fought for every inch he lost. But it was a losing battle. Chip was alone, and going away.

Two laps, one. . . .

The red car was a comet with a tail of dust. It was just a blur, going past the pits, a ball of fire whirling into the south bend. Fifteen feet behind, the black car chased it.

I saw the slide start, as Chip's momentum threw him into a skid. I saw the rear end climb, and then the dust blanketed everything.

I was running through the infield, toward the curve, when I heard the tire go.

Red was through the bend now; Red was going on to win.

Chip was all right. That was the first thing I saw. He was sitting in the car, and the car was facing down-track, resting a few inches from the upper fence. The same heavily piled dust that had made the track so treacherous had saved him from the timber.

When the tire had gone, the ridge had caught him. The car was all right, and Chip was all right. But we had lost another race.

We had hoped, even without Indianapolis, to win enough points for a Triple-A title this year. The Triple-A champion for the year is decided on points. We weren't doing so well.

Chip was out of the car, and on the other side of the fence, now. I crossed over, as soon as the track was clear.

He had his goggles off. He said, "My fault, Elm. I was trying to give 'em a last lap to remember. I didn't need that much speed."

"Let's forget it," I said. "Lots of races ahead."

"Sure," he said. "We're so rich, too." He shook his head. "All I'd need for that title would be wins in about all the races left."

I didn't answer that. We got the Speedway Four back to the pits, and ready to ship.

There was a letter from Mom at the hotel, and one from Jean. Mom said that Mr. Stevens had been to see her a couple of times, and that he was still investigating the fire—which meant that the check was still being held up.

Jean's letter was friendly and six pages long. It was also full of questions. Had I read Albert Bigelow Paine's new "authorized" biography of Mark Twain? Had I read about the furor in New York, Boston, and Philadelphia at the openings of *The Playboy of the Western World*? Had I seen the ridiculous cartoons in the paper about the suffragette parade in New York?

Chip said, "What are you frowning about? Bad news?"

157

"No," I said. "I'm just beginning to realize how ignorant I am, and it hurts." I read on.

Did I know that Elaine and Harold Adams were getting married next week?

I stopped and read that over. I put the letter away, without finishing it. Chip was sitting near the window, looking out at the street below.

I said bluntly, "Elaine is marrying your cousin."

He didn't move. He didn't even look my way. "When?"

"In a week."

He said, "They've been engaged since March. Did you know that?"

"No."

He turned to face me, then. "Well, I did. And at first, I hoped something would happen, something that would break it up. All along, I've been waiting to hear what you just told me. Maybe, it's for the best, Elm. Do you think it is?"

"I don't know," I said.

"It's money she wants, isn't it? This proves it's money—"

"I don't know," I repeated. "Chip, I'm sorry—"

"We won't talk about it," he said. He went over to pick up his hat. "I'm going out for a little walk. I'll be back in time for supper."

He wasn't back in time for supper. When he was an hour overdue, I started to look for him. Springfield wasn't a big town, but there seemed to be a lot of it.

I finally found him. He was at a corner table, his head in his arms, dead to the world. I practically carried him back to the hotel.

The next day we shipped to Chicago, for the Grand American, again. On the trip, he had nothing to say. He was pale and nervous.

It was the same track, the same boys. Different cars, and an even bigger crowd than the year before. Red Nelson wouldn't be there, I learned. I was glad of that, with Chip in his present mood.

We drew lots, this time, for starting positions. Our luck held there, our *bad* luck. We were way, way back in the line-up.

Chip was in the car, behind the wheel, and I was waiting for the signal to line-up. He looked up at me and studied me. "Remember the day we met, Elm, when I had that trouble with the Pierce?"

I nodded.

"I've sure been a millstone around your neck since that day, haven't I? You've had nothing but trouble."

"I've had a lot of fun," I said. "I like trouble."

"Maybe I'd better ride alone today, Elm," he said quietly.

I tried to read his mind. The way he'd said it scared me. "Chip," I said, "you're not going—"

He seemed puzzled at my tone. Then his face cleared. "Oh—for Pete's sake, Elm, you don't think—"

"I didn't know what to think," I said.

His smile wasn't his regular one, just a weak imitation. "No, what I meant was, this is going to be a rough one. But this one we've got to have, for a lot of reasons. This one I owe you, Elm, but it will take a lot of doing."

"I want to go along," I said. "I get nervous, just watching."

"All right," he said. "I wanted you along. I hope J. Ellington is here."

"He is," I said. "I saw him out there, a little while ago."

Chip said nothing more. The red car did his talking, after that.

We started in the eighth row, on the inside. We had fourteen good men in fast cars ahead of us, and all of them nearly as determined to win as we were.

Nearly.

I should have been nervous. Winning, from our spot in the starting line-up, against that kind of competition *would* take a lot of doing, as Chip had said.

The car was right and ready, but so were all the

160

others. Chip was ready too. I was hoping he was right.

We were under way in a flash.

Chip's smile was back, but it didn't look like the real thing. It was too tight. It was more determined than confident, more grim than cocky.

The Ryan-Adams Speedway Four was growling now, in her challenging way. Our little car with the big name would ask no quarter—and give none.

Chip made no early bid, as he had done in this same race, the year before. With a quarter of the race gone, we'd passed only Tetzlaff, when his Fiat began to sputter on the first curve, and Merz, when his Simplex threw a tire.

The little red car was winding up, but there were a lot of revs left in her yet.

With a third of the race gone, we were still in thirteenth place, as I figured it. We'd started in fifteenth. The Speedway Four's song grew higher, into the big curve near the car barns. Eddie Hearne's Case was in that curve. The gentleman racer, Eddie Hearne, who had been king of the amateurs, was a lot of man behind the wheel.

And the Case was no slouch.

Eddie wasn't ready to challenge, not yet. He was using a different strategy. His bid would come later. But he decided to make it interesting for us.

I'm glad he did. Because Chip's timing had been a shade off. We didn't realize, until we started to roll, how much of a lead we'd been sacrificing.

What a chase he gave us. The little Four's thunder grew higher and higher as we chased Eddie's big job out of the bend. Into a long stretch, now, dotted with cars far ahead, cars that grew bigger and bigger. We weren't gaining an inch on the Case.

The stretch was nearly over now. Cars were going by, but *backward,* and to our right. We were climbing. I counted them, as they flashed by. I figured we were riding ninth, as we hit the curve. The Case still led us; the Case seemed to have more stuff.

I looked over at Chip, and saw the smile. It was almost the old smile, but there was still the tightness in it. I felt the red car surge. Chip had been holding out on me. There were lots of revs left in our baby, even now.

It was a hard curve, and a rough one. The Case went right down the middle of it, jolting, drifting high, toward the right edge. Eddie planned to cut at the edge, I knew, and power down when he hit the peak of it.

Chip rode low, to the left. He would need a lot of wrist to stay down there. He fought hard against the deck sway. We started to climb, and Chip cut, just a fraction. We found the groove again, as the Case kept sliding high.

It would take some timing. It would take some judgment, and all the nerve in the world. We had to play it fair. We weren't going to pull any rough stuff, not on Eddie Hearne.

Chip's foot found the floor.

The Ryan-Adams responded like the thoroughbred she was. We shot past the Case, seconds before she started to come down again. Chip had gone by, on the inside, allowing him the legal clearance. It was sweet and neat and clean, and I was proud of him.

Eddie wasn't out of it, not by a long shot. I thought we'd been making time chasing him. It was slow, compared to this. The Case wasn't the car on a curve ours was, but Eddie knew all there was to know about the straightaway. He came down out of the bend like an avenging angel, and camped on our trail.

To our right, another car went by backwards. We were riding seventh. Eddie was riding eighth. He was also riding our deck. Then Chip threw away the anchor.

The motor noise was lost in the wind, the tremor of the floor boards was like a minor earthquake. I stole a glance behind. The Case didn't seem to be losing any ground. This was a straight run, and the Case a straightaway sweetheart.

It began to close the gap. It was crowding us again, as the next curve loomed.

Chip played this one the same way, low, without any broadsiding. He picked up some precious yardage. It was practically an S curve, and he picked up more yardage on the reverse turn.

And that's the game we played. That's the only chance we had against that high-geared Case, making up on the curves what we had lost on the stretches.

Other cars went by, backwards. We came into the home stretch in second place. The number one car was way ahead. If Hearne hadn't met our challenge when he did, we'd have been out of this one. If the car ahead had our speed, we'd still be out of this one.

It didn't have. It was Cobe's Jackson, and we caught him a good half mile from the flag.

We had come out of the last curve with a substantial lead on Eddie. But now that lead was being whittled down to nothing.

We passed Cobe, and moved over, to give Eddie room. Our red job was giving all she had, to the last rev.

I thought of the year before, when we'd caught

DePalma in this stretch. I looked back, and it seemed the Case wasn't gaining. I continued to look back and saw that I was wrong.

He wasn't gaining by much, but it was steady —and he had a half mile to catch us in.

It was like one of those dreams where someone is chasing you, someone always just a step behind, someone who never gets tired. Eddie was even with our rear wheels, with the deck.

The road here was solidly lined with fans, and they were going wild. Ahead, I could see the finish line. The Case was even with our seat now, inching forward, pulling up to the back of the hood.

I could see the flag, raised. The Case was pulling up. I sighted directly to my left, and saw it wasn't quite abreast, not yet, even allowing for its longer hood.

I saw him come more directly in line—as the flag dropped.

As the sound of the motor grew quieter, as the compression slowed us down, Chip asked, "Did we do it, Elm?"

"I don't know," I said.

Eddie still rode alongside. His mechanic called over, "Ten more feet, and we'd have had you."

"I thought you did have us," Chip said. "I lost my youth, back there."

For the second time, we'd won the Grand American. For the first time, that season, we'd won a race.

It wasn't the last one. We went up to Palmyra, for the Midwest dirt track title. Red was there, among others. The Adams Special sounded better than ever. Red set a qualifying lap that stood for three years.

It was Springfield all over again. Only this time in reverse. Red made a monkey of the field. He lapped the local boys, and he had a good quarter lap lead on Chip, with five miles to go.

Again Chip's only chance was to make it up on the turns. In four laps, he cut the lead down to two hundred feet. With a lap to go, he was practically out of it.

Red barreled by, flame tipping his tail pipe, the motor sounding like the best in the world at that moment. Red went sliding into the south turn, sliding, sliding, sliding. . . .

As I said, it was Springfield in reverse.

The black job never stopped sliding, even when it hit the fence. Timber was outlined against the sky—and Chip went by below to win.

Red came out of it all right, and so did his car, outside of the right front wheel.

In the pits, Chip said, "We need higher compression in this baby. We need a high-lift cam."

"You won," I said. "You beat Red."

"No, I didn't. He beat himself, just like I did at Springfield. But he's got more stuff under the hood now, Elm. And he isn't the only one. We'll have to tear her down."

Chip had recovered some of his old good humor, but not enough, not nearly enough. There were moments when he was quiet and moody. Elaine was on his mind, I knew. Despite her obvious snobbery, she was a memory difficult to erase.

St. Paul wasn't much of a contest. It was Triple-A sanctioned, this year, but the big boys didn't make it. They were getting ready for the loaded August calendar.

Chip had enough under the hood for St. Paul. He won all the races he entered, the ten, the fifteen, the twenty-five. It paid very little.

At home, we tore down the Speedway Four, and installed the new camshaft. We had the head planed, for more compression. We counted our money.

"If only that insurance check would come through," I said.

"Why don't we look up this Stevens fellow and see what's new on that?" Chip suggested.

We met him at his hotel, but he had nothing for us. He said, "Arson has been established, plainly enough. The company isn't paying—until—all possible *interested* suspects are cleared."

"That means us? That *interested* means us?" Chip asked.

Stevens expelled his breath. "Nothing personal, Mr. Adams. I'm telling you what the company has ordered. My own opinion is not necessarily the same, but I work under orders." He paused. "I'm sure that, before I'm through, you'll be glad the company kept me on the investigation."

"You're sure?" I asked. "You've discovered something?"

His face was a blank. "I've discovered nothing I can prove. You gentlemen will have to be patient."

On the way home, Chip said, "I think he's a stuffed shirt. I don't think he could find a ton of coal in a basement."

"He's working for a big outfit," I argued. "He's got a responsible job. We may as well string along with him."

"May as well?" Chip said. "We've got to."

I saw Jean that evening. She was more wonderful than ever. I told her about the Grand American, about Springfield and St. Paul and Meadow Bay. We never did get around to talking about that biography of Mark Twain. But she didn't seem to mind.

We shipped to Arco the next day. Red was

there again. He won the fifteen miler, Chip the ten. They were both in the twenty-five mile feature.

In the pits, I told Chip, "Race to win. But don't make it personal. Don't let that temper of yours lose you a race, or endanger the lives of the other boys out there."

"All right, Uncle Elm," he said, with mock gravity.

"I'm serious, Chip," I said.

"I'll be careful, Elm," he said, and he was serious, too, now.

This "being careful" is a comparative term. Compared to Springfield, he was careful. Compared to taming lions or deep-sea diving, he wasn't. He was being as careful as his trade permitted.

Of course, it was only twenty-five miles. In any race, you can only die once.

He and Red tangled, right from the start. At ten miles, it began to look as though Red still had more than we did. In any event, he was running away.

Chip chased him grimly. Chip did some of the finest wheeling of his career, and chased Red all the way to the checkered flag.

In the pits, he sat in the car, saying nothing.

I said, "He's got too much. He's got a faster car."

Chip shook his head. "You know he hasn't, Elm."

I said, "You trying to tell me he's a better driver?"

Chip looked startled. "Of course not! It's the gas we're using, Elm. Too much ping. With this higher compression, we'll have to hop up our gas, some way."

I breathed a sigh of relief. "For a minute, I thought he had you jinxed." I should have known, of course. A man who had beaten Oldfield and DePalma and Hearne wasn't going to worry too much about Red Nelson. But Red had won again.

It was the next day that Eddie told me about the Atwater Run, two weeks off. They were giving away a lot of money at that one. I told Chip about it at supper that night.

He shook his head. "It's not Triple-A sanctioned. They're running at Kelsington, the same day. We need the points, Elm. If I can beat Red at Kelsington, I can tie him for points, and—"

"Red won't be there," I said. "He'll be at Atwater. So will a lot of others. It's an outlaw meet, Chip, but it pays in blue chips."

He looked doubtful. "Who's financing it?"

"That's why we're going," I said. "The man who will hand out the checks and the cup is a man we want to meet. He'll have to talk to us, Chip, if only to congratulate us."

He stared at me.

"A man named J. Ellington Duffy," I finished.

170

Chip gulped. "Maybe it's invitational. If it is—"

"It isn't," I said, "but there's an entry fee, and it will cut us way down."

"We'll make it up," he said. "We'll make it up out of the purse, out of first money." He shook his head. "Elm, I can see him shaking my hand, right now. I can see him listening, while I explain how much he needs us, if he's going to stay in business."

"I can't quite see it," I said, "knowing the boys who'll be there."

Chip didn't answer. But his smile was a cocky smile. His smile didn't have any remembrance of Elaine in it.

We increased the octane count of our gas. And in a garage near Atwater, we pulled the Speedway apart again. Not that she needed it, but we wanted to be sure. We didn't want to miss this one if we could help it.

J. Ellington Duffy was around during the pre-liminary runs. We saw him from time to time, but he couldn't seem to see us. The few times we were close to him, he was busily engaged in conversation with somebody else.

"Why don't you wring my neck?" Chip asked me. "Why don't you send me out on my own?"

"I need your moderating influence," I said. "I need your thoughtful judgment."

When we had the Speedway Four ready, we made a tour of the route to be used. All the roads leading into the run were now barricaded, and the boys were trying it out.

About halfway through it, we overtook the Adams Special. Red wasn't alone; Harold Adams was riding with him.

We moved by. Chip kept his eyes straight ahead, and so did I. Chip stepped on the red baby's tail, and she jumped in response. The Special didn't follow. Red was taking no chances with the president of the Adams Engine Company.

It was that afternoon we met Elaine. She was sitting in the Mercedes, in front of the hotel, and she looked happy. She looked like a girl who had married a quarter of a million dollars.

"Chip Adams," she said. "Oh, it's good to see you, Chip. And you, Elmer."

Chip's face showed nothing I could read. He said politely, "You look well, Elaine. You look happy."

I couldn't read her face, either. She said, "I am happy, Chip. I'm on my honeymoon, my delayed honeymoon. After the race, Harold and I are going to New York, for a month, and then—"

The voice went chattering on. I wondered if there were malice in it. I wondered how Chip was taking it. You couldn't tell, by looking at him.

Maybe, I thought, he can see now, and he's grateful. Maybe, this is the best thing that could have happened. His eyes didn't leave her face, all the time she was talking.

His voice was level, as he said, "Well, we have to be getting along, Elaine. I'm glad I saw you."

When we were out of earshot, he said, "Harold's business must be good if he can leave it for a month to go to New York."

"Maybe it's a business trip," I said. "Harold's the kind who would combine business with pleasure."

Chip had no answer to that.

We made another tour of the layout that afternoon. It was a long run, with a few hills, with some really treacherous turns, and narrow all the way. As we traveled it, we studied it. Chip's comments were made in a flat, dead voice. His face showed no emotion at all.

Starting positions were determined by lots. We drew the fourth row, on the outside. Red was behind us, in the sixth row.

Ahead of us were Hughes, Tetzlaff and Dawson, Wilcox and Mulford and Jenkins. To our left was Merz, in his Stutz. The sun was blazing from an unclouded sky; the road would be hard and dusty.

The motors were turning over. The starter went down the rows, past us, all the way to the end. Chip said, "We can't miss, forever, can we, Elm? This one should be our big break. Duffy can't ignore us, after this one."

"He's had a lot of practice, ignoring us," I answered. "Maybe it's a habit he can't break."

Chip shook his head. "Not this time. I feel it, Elm. Our luck's due for a change."

I didn't feel it, not at all. But maybe my intuition wasn't as sound as his.

The starter was satisfied; the cars were moving forward. To our left, Merz waved, and we waved back. Overhead, the sun was hotter than ever.

Past the solid banks of spectators, the pace rising, the tail pipes growling higher. Past the judge's stand, past J. Ellington Duffy, in a suit no less bright than the sun. Past the cup, which seemed brighter than the sun, a mammoth, hand-wrought beauty of a cup.

Past the edge of town, out onto the narrow, unbanked ribbon of hard dust that comprised the Atwater Run.

The red baby sounded right and ready, her song sweetly even. To our left, Merz' Stutz surged ahead. Chip met the challenge, and we went gunning into the first curve.

I don't remember the complete sequence of that race, but I remember that first battle with Merz. We paced it out on the turn, Merz had the advantage there. The curve was to the left, and the Stutz had the left side of the road. What bank there was, from the edge to the crown, favored Merz.

We were on the reverse slope, to the right of the crown. Chip's wrists were all that made a challenge possible there. Merz led us out of the turn by ten feet.

He gave us a race, the first quarter of the run. The Stutz seemed to be geared to the road, a sure-footed sweetheart of a car. Chip trailed by a few feet, waiting for a break.

Down the narrow stretch, we trailed, and into the second curve. I looked down at Chip's right foot, and it seemed very close to the floor boards. We were riding seventh.

Into another stretch, and the Speedway Four was winding up, now. I felt that tremor in the floor boards, the jolt of the rough, hard road. We pulled alongside the Stutz, and started to move by.

The Stutz moved right along with us.

Chip revved our baby right up to her peak, and again we began to move by. Slowly, though, inch by stubborn inch—and another curve was coming up.

We were gaining. We were past, but under full power—as we hit the turn. The car seemed to possess a mind of its own, as it hurtled toward the ditch, as Chip fought grimly to regain the crown of the road. For a tortuous second, we teetered there, on the rocky edge of the gully.

Chip was leaning far to the left, pulling the wheel that way. Then we were slamming down, across the crown, under control.

I breathed again.

I don't remember passing anyone for a while, after that, but we must have. Because, with half the race run, we were in fourth place.

Ahead, there were no cars in sight. Behind us, a black speck was growing bigger and bigger.

We breasted a small hill, and there was Tetzlaff's Fiat, throwing a regular hail of pebbles onto our cowl, raising a storm of dust. Ahead, the road was straight, and downhill. The Speedway Four was wide open.

So was the Fiat, but we had more under the hood, that day. We went by, crowding the left edge of the road, riding the narrow rim of the gully, like a tightrope.

We rode third, and we were logging. Behind, the black speck had become a black car. It was the Adams Special, I could see now. Red was on our trail.

The wind was burning us. The roar of the motor was dim, in the wind-howl, but the vibration of our new compression ratio was making itself evident.

It had added speed, all right, that new ratio, but we had sacrificed a lot of smoothness for it.

Chip's eyes squinted almost shut as a long, sweeping curve took us directly into the glare of the sun. If his vision was as impaired as mine, he wasn't seeing anything. But he didn't cut down a single m.p.h.

Ahead, there was a blanket of dust, dimming the sun. It was the car in second place, but whose it was, I couldn't see. Chip made no challenge in that glare; the motor throb cut lower as he eased on the throttle.

The blanket of dust was moving to the right, now. We were on a curve. We were turning away from the glare, and I could see it was Hughes' Mercer.

Chip's right foot probed, as we swung out of the curve. The Mercer moved right with us, but only for the moment. The red car had the acceleration. In five hundred yards Chip settled that duel. We were riding in second place.

I stole a glance behind. There was another car passing Hughes, the black car that had been a speck. It was life-size now.

"It's Red Nelson, coming up," I shouted at Chip. "And he's logging."

Chip's smile was there. "Let me know when he makes his bid."

"He's practically making it now," I said. "You've got thirty feet on him."

Chip nodded, but the car maintained its pace. The black car came closer, and Chip made no move. He waited, waited until I said, "He's starting to go by."

The red baby seemed to lunge.

The black car came up even with the seat, and beyond, and that's where it stayed. We were wide open, and he had all we had. For there was no change I could notice, as we hurtled along.

It was a narrow road, as I've said, and the two cars spanned it right to the edges. If we came to a curve, if that haze of dust, far ahead was another car. . . .

If it was, it was the car in first place.

We were gaining, I suddenly realized. The black car was moving backward, slowly fading.

The car ahead kept getting bigger—and then flame poured from its tail pipe, and a black cloud of smoke belched out. It was slowing. It was stopping, and we still didn't have the clearance to cut to the left; Red crowded our back wheels.

I saw Chip tense, as he sized up the situation. I felt an almost negligible surge of acceleration—and then Chip cut viciously to the left, directly in front of Red.

There was the sharp stench of unburned gas and

oil, a frightening glimpse of the deck of the stalled car, only inches from us. I twisted around to see Red going for the brakes.

Then we were clear, and in first place.

Maybe it was legal, and maybe it wasn't. But we had owed Red that one. Chip didn't play any more; he souped the Ryan-Adams right up to her limit. Behind, Red didn't seem to be losing much ground.

There were two curves left, one of them bad, one long and gradual. We got through the long one, all right, with Red crowding us, trailing us by no more than five feet all the way through.

We maintained the five feet through the stretch that followed. We carried it into the last bend, the nasty one. It was a sharp curve to the left, and Chip played it to the left, using what bank the drainage slope afforded him.

He cut before going in, planning on a power spin, halfway through. Red came into it under power.

Red went high, sliding. Then he cut down, across our path. He was beyond us, above us. It was a replica of his trick at Meadow Bay.

I saw the nose of his car slamming down. I could almost count the cells in his radiator. I didn't look at Chip for his reaction. I couldn't take my eyes from the onrushing radiator.

Red was making it a test of nerves. He should have realized this was the wrong time for that. For there was nobody behind, this time. Chip stayed in his groove. Red must have realized, in the last second, that Chip wouldn't be scared.

For he jerked the wheel savagely, and the long black car went sliding back across the road toward the right edge, the deck low, and swinging to the left.

We made it. We cleared that careening deck by inches, and barreled on, all alone in first place.

I glanced back to see the black job swing in a complete gilhooley, facing back toward the road it had traveled. I saw the tire go, and the car lurch.

Red didn't leave the road, but he was out of it, out of the money.

There wasn't another car in sight as we rode down on the checkered flag, on the cheering crowd around the finish line.

This should be it, the end of the long trail.

It was a big cup, and the smile on J. Ellington Duffy's broad face looked good to me. But there wasn't any smile in his voice. He gave us the cup and the first prize money and his congratulations as quickly and as matter-of-factly as a bank teller paying off. Then he turned his back on us, and was lost in the fans who crowded around. Chip looked at me, and I looked at Chip. Then Chip looked away. Neither of us said a word.

When we got back to the hotel, an hour later, he still hadn't spoken.

He went in first, to take his bath. When he came out, he said, "We've been kicked around a lot, this year, Elm. It's about time we did something about it."

"We're doing all we can," I said. "I can't think of anything we've overlooked." I picked up my robe, and headed for the bathroom.

I hadn't finished my bath when Chip came in, fully dressed. "I'm going to look up the trains," he said. "I'm going down to the station."

I nodded, and he left.

I was dressing, when the messenger brought the note. It read, simply:

Elm:
Saw a chance, and grabbed a train for New York. Maybe it's a crazy idea, and maybe not. I won't tell you why until I know.

Chip.

New York . . . Elaine was going to New York. But that was dead, or should be. I hoped he didn't plan to break *that* up. Even if he could, she wasn't for him. She wasn't nearly good enough for him, I knew now.

I made all the arrangements for shipping the Speedway Four home, and followed it home, alone.

There was a wire from Chip, two hours after I arrived home. "Wire me two hundred" it read, and I wired him two hundred. I hoped he wasn't using it to break up a marriage.

It was a restless time. I fiddled with the Ryan-Adams a little, just to keep busy, but my heart wasn't in it. I wanted to see Jean, but she was out of town.

It was a hot afternoon, and I was sitting on the porch, reading the paper the boy had just left. It made very interesting reading, that day, particularly the headline news.

"Well, Rube," somebody said, "you might say *hello.*"

Chip stood on the walk, his eyes shining, a brief case in his right hand. The carriage that had brought him was leaving the yard.

"I didn't hear you," I said. "The paper—this news—"

"I've got news, too," he said, "and papers for you to sign." He took a deep breath. "We're in, Elm. You and I and Ellington Duffy are in the automobile business. You see, while I was at the station—"

His voice went on and on, explaining. I don't remember the exact words, any more, but he'd seen J. Ellington Duffy, when he'd gone to the station, and had heard him buy a ticket for New York. On a hunch, Chip had bought a ticket for the same train.

182

"I talked to him on the train," he told me, "and I made an appointment to see him again in New York. Elm, I talked like I never talked before in my life. You see, Harold was there, and Harold had the same idea I had." He shook his head. "But somebody, last spring, mailed J. Ellington one of those announcements of ours, and—" He looked at me with sudden suspicion. "Hey, you—"

"Guilty," I admitted. "And I'm glad to know we've got Duffy behind us. I think we'll do all right, Chip. I know we will."

"And now," he said, "what was in that newspaper that's so important."

I showed him the headline—ENGINE EXECUTIVE INDICTED FOR ARSON. I said, "We underrated Mike Stevens. He's nailed Jim Masker, nailed him cold."

There were some years after that, some other exciting years. Bad and good and some I don't remember. There was always Jean, for all the years. There was our car, which I won't name, because that would be unethical advertising. But if you drive one in its field, the chances are you're driving ours. We have led the field since 1920.

Chip never married but he's been a second father to our kids, Jean's and mine, or maybe it would be more accurate to say he's been a brother. He takes their side and he argues with them against me when I try to point out why they should go into the business.

Since we left the jet age and went into the space age, my kids all talk rockets, rockets, rockets, and who will be first to really establish a home on those beckoning planets. Crazy talk; kids don't have the proper respect for tradition the way they used to have. Traveling on the ground is much too slow for them.

Well, what was good enough for my folks is good enough for me. Maybe Chip won't grow up, but I have. It will be a long time before you see the last automobile, you can bet on that.

For that matter, as Mom says, it will be a long time before you see the last horse.

But I don't really fight with my kids. I argue a little, but kids will be kids, and I pray that the day *never* comes when our kids will be satisfied with what *we* had.

When that day comes, you can say *Good-by, America.*

Gault

II. Thunder